THE NAME OF THE GAME IS A KIDNAPPING

KEIGO HIGASHINO

TRANSLATED BY JAN MITSUKO CASH

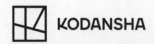 KODANSHA

The Name of the Game Is a Kidnapping
A VERTICAL Book

Publication rights for this English edition arranged with Kobunsha Co., Ltd., Tokyo through Tuttle-Mori Agency, Inc., Tokyo.

English language version produced by Kodansha USA Publishing, LLC, 2023.

Originally published in Japan as *GAME NO NA WA YUKAI* by Kobunsha Co., Ltd., Tokyo, 2002.

Previously issued in English in hardcover in 2017.

ISBN 978-1-64729-321-5

Printed in the United States of America

First Paperback Edition

Kodansha USA Publishing, LLC
451 Park Avenue South, 7th Floor
New York, NY 10016
www.kodansha.us

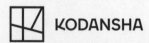

KODANSHA

THE NAME OF THE GAME IS A KIDNAPPING

1

The moment she mentioned the word "marriage," I lost interest in the woman. I could only see her large chest, her slim legs, and even her smooth skin as the parts of a mannequin.

I gave her an unamused look and then got out of bed. I put on my boxers that I had tossed aside and fixed my rumpled hair while looking in the mirror.

"What's with that face?" The woman raised herself halfway up, flipping her long hair. "You don't have to be so blunt and make such a sour face."

I wasn't even in the mood to reply. I looked at the alarm clock. Five minutes before eight in the morning. Just the right time. I switched off the alarm that would've gone off in five minutes.

"I'm already twenty-seven, okay?" the woman added. "You could stand to listen to a little of that."

"I told you I've never thought about marriage," I said with my back still facing her.

"You said you don't think about it a lot. Not that you never think about it."

"Is that right."

I thought it might be this way, but when I see through something, I get bored. I started doing pushups by the bed. I was careful about the rhythm, and when I flexed, I exhaled. Just like my gym instructor told me.

"Hey, are you mad?"

I didn't answer. I'd lose count of my pushups. Twenty-eight, twenty-nine, thirty, then it got a little harder.

"Then let me ask, what do you plan on doing with me?"

I went down on the forty-second pushup. I rolled on the floor like that and thrust both my legs under the bed. Setup for sit-ups.

"I didn't really have any plans. I liked you. I thought I wanted to sleep with you. So I did. That's all there is to it."

"Meaning that you weren't thinking of marriage."

"I thought I told you from the start. I wasn't thinking about anything like that. Unlike you, I wasn't thinking about it at all, and I don't plan on starting now."

"And if I say that I don't like that?"

"It's useless. You'll need to find a guy who'll think about marriage. It should be easy for you to find one."

"You're saying you're tired of me?"

"It's not that. We've only been dating for three months. But when there's a difference in opinion, you can only give up."

The woman sank into silence. I couldn't tell what she was thinking. She was a woman with a lot of pride, so she wouldn't say anything unbecoming. While she was thinking, I started my sit-ups. Since turning thirty, it'd become easier for my belly to put on fat. I couldn't get away with not doing this every morning.

The woman said, "I'm going home," and got down from the bed. It was pretty much the answer I'd predicted.

While I did sit-ups, she put on her clothes. A black dress. Without fixing her makeup, she took her bag in hand.

"You're not getting any calls from me."

With those words, she left the room. I'd heard her voice still on my side by the bed.

She had a magnificent body, but it couldn't be helped. It was true I was struck by that physique, but I didn't feel like living with her for a lifetime. Of course, I could have used the technique of hinting at marriage as appropriate to keep dating her. Then, if the time came that I'd actually gotten bored, I'd just have to talk about breaking up. But doing it like that didn't suit me. It wasn't because it'd be on my conscience, but because it'd be a bother. I'd been in more romantic relationships than I could count now, including ones that were sustained through accumulating lies and compromises, but I knew deep down that it would do me no good.

By the time I'd taken a shower and shaved at the washbasin, I was no longer thinking about the woman who had left. Instead, the names of two others floated into my head. One was a model in the making, the other was just an office lady. I knew the phone numbers for both of them, but I'd never called them. I'd gotten a call from the model. The one I liked was really the office lady, but when we went out drinking before, I got the feeling that there wasn't a lot of hope. I couldn't find it in myself to do this and that and everything possible to woo her. I didn't think she was worth it, and more importantly, I didn't have the time.

I fried some ham and eggs, toasted bread, and warmed up canned soup for my breakfast. Lately, I was lacking vegetables. There had to be some cauliflower in the refrigerator so I decided I'd have a gratin with a lot of that in it tonight.

Changing into my suit, I booted up my computer and checked my email. Several items dealing with work. The rest of it was all trivial stuff. There was one from a hostess at a club I went to the other day. I deleted it without reading it.

By the time I left the room, it was a little past nine. That meant I'd taken more than an hour since waking up. I still had a long way to go using my time wisely. I walked at a brisk pace to the subway station. It took seven minutes.

My work was in Minato Ward. The ninth and tenth floors of a fifteen-story building were occupied by Cyberplan. I got off the elevator at the tenth floor.

When I got to my desk, a piece of paper that said, "Come to my office –Kozuka," was on my computer. I put down my bag and headed on down the hallway.

The president's office door had been left open. When it was closed, you weren't to try to meet with the president except on very urgent business. If it was open, it meant that you could go in freely. It was Kozuka's policy.

Kozuka was in the midst of discussing something with a female employee. When he noticed me, he cut off the conversation.

"I'll leave the rest to you. Anyway, don't use that designer anymore," Kozuka told the woman. She answered that she understood and left the room. When she passed by me, she gave me a slight bow.

"If I'm not mistaken, she's in charge of producing a new game."

"Well, games are hard." Kozuka closed a file that had been laid out on his desk. "Please close the door."

It seemed he was preparing for a discussion about either a large amount of easy money or something serious. I closed the door and approached his desk.

"We got word from Nissei Automobile," the forty-five-year-old president said.

"They finally made a decision? Then we need to arrange for the first set of meetings. I can make an opening any time this week."

However, Kozuka remained seated with a long look. "That's not it."

"This isn't about the automobile park?"

"It is."

"Then, do you mean that it'll take some time before the decision is made?"

"No, the decision has been made. I just got word."

"Then?"

"It's been canceled."

"What?" Unable to comprehend his statement, I took a step toward him. No, I understood the meaning of it. It was just so idiotic that I couldn't bring myself to believe it.

"Canceled. The automobile park plan is back to being a blank slate."

"But…how could that be?"

I wanted to believe that Kozuka was telling a bad joke. But I didn't sense that possibility in his expression. I felt like my blood was coursing backwards through my veins and like my whole body temperature had risen by several degrees.

"I can't believe it either," Kozuka shook his head. "That it was canceled after making it this far."

"What happened? Please explain the situation to me."

"I'm going to ask about the details tonight—we've got a meeting then. Even so, they might just give us a formal notice."

"Is it just going to be completely scrapped? Or do they mean that the chances of implementing it are low?"

"The chances of it are zero. The concept of the automobile park's been rejected."

I balled my right hand into a fist and struck the palm of my left. "Why, after getting this far…"

"The supervisor was also confused."

"Of course. Considering how much time was used up for this project…"

"The person also said they would guarantee all the funds we've used until now."

"I wouldn't think it'd be a matter of money though."

"Well, that may be the case." Kozuka scratched the side of his nose.

I stuck both my hands into my pockets and paced in front of the desk. "Nissei Automobile was planning to announce a new car and wanted to launch an extensive campaign. While they were at it, they wanted to improve the image of domestic cars. They hoped for something like a car show, but not just a plain exhibit. To that end, they could use our help. Isn't that what they said?"

"Of course it is."

"Instead of contacting a major firm, they asked a mid-sized company like ours because, putting aside the budget, they hoped for a novel idea, right?"

"It was exactly that."

"But then when the current plan was settled, and all that we needed was the go sign, they got cold feet, is that what you're saying? The world-renowned Nissei."

"Well, don't get mad like that. I know it's one of the largest jobs we've ever had and that you were fired up. But the client was the one who ran away so there's nothing we can do. It won't be the last time."

"I can't stand having these things happen, even from time to time."

"The one who's most annoyed about this is me. I have to redo our business plan all over again. Nissei says that it's preparing to turn over another job, but we can't expect much from them."

"They're just going to ask us to make another commercial with an idol anyway. May I also come with you to tonight's meeting?"

"I'd rather you didn't." Kozuka stuck out his right palm. "If you go, you might fight with the other side. If we quietly suck it up, we'll draw some favor."

That merchant-like thinking was very Kozuka. He wasn't a creator, but a manager, I realized anew. After taking a long breath, I asked him, "Is the project team dissolved?"

"That's what'll end up happening. Tonight, once I hear about the situation I'll email you, so based on that, write a directive to the members."

"There will undoubtedly be others who'll be even more upset."

"Probably." Kozuka shrugged his shoulders.

I stayed at the office until late in the afternoon that day, but in the end I wasn't getting much work done. *Why?* The sentiment kept bubbling up in my chest. I left early and headed towards my usual sports gym.

I rode on the cycles for nearly forty minutes and sweated a ton, but felt far from exhilarated. Feeling desperate, I went to train on the machines, but my body just felt sluggish. After completing three quarters of my normal regimen, I took a shower.

My cellphone went off just as I left the gym. I had some recollection of the number on the display, but I couldn't remember exactly from where.

"Sakuma? It's me, Kozuka."

"Yes, president. Did you finish your talk with Nissei?"

"It's over. And so I have something I want to talk to you a bit about. I'm in Roppongi right now, could you come out here?"

"Yes, I can. Where's the place?"

"It's 'Sabine.' You know it, right?"

"I do. I'll be there in thirty minutes."

After I hung up, a taxi came by with perfect timing. I raised my hand.

Sabine was a place a certain health food company managed for tax reasons. I'd been taken there by Kozuka a few times. It was excessively spacious and flashy and had a lot of hostesses. The interior, which was made up like a decorated cake, was the kind of affair that made you fed up just looking at it. I always thought that if only they would leave it to me I could make a place far more refined with half the money.

I got out of the taxi and got into the elevator of a building nearby.

A tall blonde and a man clad in black stood near the entrance. The male staffer extended an excessively polite greeting and the

11

blonde welcomed me in halting Japanese.

"President Kozuka is here, right?"

"Yes, he is present tonight."

The establishment split to the right and left at the entrance. If you went left, that was where the hall was, and to the right were the counter seats. I was guided to the right, but Kozuka wasn't waiting at the counter. In the back, there was a private room, a VIP space for special guests. But it wasn't like Kozuka spent that much here. It was just that he could make some requests through a Dietmember connection. Even now, Kozuka was the brains for that politician's image strategy.

In the private room, Kozuka was accompanied by two hostesses and drinking a Hennessy on the rocks. When he saw my face, he raised his hand slightly.

"Sorry for calling you out here."

"No, it was already on my mind."

Kozuka nodded as though to say, *Of course.*

The hostess asked how I wanted my drink, so I answered, *Straight.* The VIP room also had a dedicated counter. The hostess went to get a brandy glass from there. She filled it with Hennessy, but I didn't feel like tasting it yet.

"Sorry, but we have some business just for the two of us," Kozuka said, at which the two hostesses left with forced smiles.

"So then?" I tried asking.

"Right, I got the gist of the situation. It seems the cancelation was decided at the board meeting the other day."

"I understood that. I want to know the reason."

"The reason"—Kozuka chinked the ice together in his glass— "is that they can't expect effects commensurate to the large scale. In a nutshell, that's what it comes down to."

"Can't expect? Whose call was it? Didn't we temporarily have the green light because they judged it would be effective?"

"You won't be convinced as long as I talk around the bush, so I'll be straight with you. The one who protested the automobile park was Mr. Katsuragi, the newly appointed executive vice president."

"When you say Katsuragi, you mean the chairman's son?"

"Mr. Katsutoshi Katsuragi. Apparently he proposed rethinking everything from the beginning."

"So the plan we worked on for weeks disappeared on some rich kid's whim?"

"That man isn't just a rich kid. After frontline stints in their sales and promotions divisions, he beefed up on marketing techniques at their American branch. He might have been appointed as the EVP before he even turned fifty because he's the chairman's son, but he has no reputation at all for being subpar."

"Mr. Kozuka, did you meet him tonight?"

"I did. He had the gaze of a raptor. And he didn't laugh even once." Maybe it was because Kozuka felt incredibly overwhelmed, but he gulped down the brandy in his glass in one go.

"How awful. Enter a despot."

I reached for my glass too.

"Mr. Katsuragi said he would give us one more chance."

"Oh." With my glass in hand, I looked back at the youthful president's face. "Different story, then. Let's rework the plan. This time we'll come up with something he can't complain about."

"Of course, that's what I intend, but he gave us two conditions. One was to highlight how they're dealing with environmental issues. And it's not just about exhaust fumes and energy conservation. He apparently wants to let it be known that Nissei takes environmental protections into consideration even within their manufacturing process."

"That seems like it'll become tedious. So, what was the other condition?"

"Yes, about that." Kozuka poured himself a glass. He didn't try to make eye contact.

"What's the other condition?" I asked again.

Kozuka breathed a small sigh before opening his mouth. "That we need to replace the staff wholesale. In particular that we should switch out the leader, Shunsuke Sakuma."

Even though my name had come up, I didn't immediately understand what he was saying. No, it was hard to take in *because* my name had come up. "He wants me out of the picture?"

"Apparently, Mr. Katsuragi conducted a thorough review of your jobs until now. The results pointed to a certain conclusion. Remember, I'm not the one saying this. It's the words of Executive Vice President Katsuragi."

"Please tell me."

"Mr. Sakuma's way of doing things may be striking and attract a lot of attention in the short term, but he is missing a view of the long term. His ideas are simple and easy to get, but he is unable to tune into people's hearts. The notion of building a pseudo-amusement park for a new car's campaign is hardly novel, and the superficiality of his way of thinking is evident. Nissei's customers purchase not only our cars, but pride. None would go to an amusement park to be proud. I want to entrust this next opportunity to someone who is able to figure out everything two steps ahead—those were Mr. Katsuragi's words."

I was cemented in place still holding my glass. It was as though rage and humiliation were filling my entire body. I felt as though if I said anything, I'd yell, and if I moved, I'd throw my glass.

"Did you miss that?" Kozuka asked.

I shook my head. "Basically, he said Sakuma from Cyberplan is incompetent…"

"He didn't go that far. He's just saying that you don't match up with his policies."

"Isn't that the same thing? It's because Mr. Katsuragi thinks of himself as the best." I gulped down my brandy. I felt the sensation of it moving down from my throat to my stomach.

"Anyway, all our firm can do is accept the conditions. Tomorrow, I'm talking to Sugimoto."

"Is Sugimoto my replacement?"

"That's how it's going to be."

"Sugimoto the concert guy, huh?" I laughed. Out of sarcasm, and as a bluff.

"That'll be all."

"I understand." I stood up.

"Why don't you stay and drink for a bit. My policy is to keep company with a guy who needs to get wasted."

"Please don't be unreasonable." I raised both my hands slightly to beg mercy.

Kozuka nodded, muttering that it might well have been unreasonable as he lowered his glass.

When I left Sabine, I didn't feel like going straight home, so I stopped by a bar I'd been to several times before. I swigged bourbon on the rocks in a seat at the end of the counter, but I couldn't shake off the feeling I'd just swallowed lead. *He is unable to tune into people's hearts; the superficiality of his way of thinking is evident; I want to entrust this next opportunity to someone who is able to figure out everything two steps ahead*—all of the words I'd just heard were managing to wreck my inner balance.

Give me a break, I thought. It had been four years since I was headhunted from a major ad agency, and since then there hadn't been a single product I'd worked on that I hadn't been able to sell. Whether it was a thing or a person, treasure or garbage, I had pride that I'd sold it. There was no way someone who couldn't tune into people's hearts could do that.

I was still in the worst of moods, but my head started feeling a little foggy, so I decided to leave that establishment, too. I went out to the street and hailed a cab.

"Where to?" the driver asked me.

Kayabacho, I was supposed to answer. Because my condo was there. But I was unexpectedly hit by a strange urge. A whim, you might call it. I heard myself respond, "Go to Denenchofu." I added, "You know that mansion of Nissei Automobile's chairman, Shotaro Katsuragi? It's near there."

"Yes, that big mansion." The driver knew the address.

2

It was a stupidly huge Western-style house. If it weren't for the nameplate, it could've easily been mistaken for some institution. The gate that seemed big enough for a semi to pass through had doors that were decorated with intricate patterns. Garage shutters flanked the gate. It seemed like four cars could easily fit in there, even Mercedes-Benzes or Rolls-Royces. Just over the wall were all kinds of trees planted like a jungle so that you really had to struggle to glimpse the roof of the main building, which seemed awfully far away, too. It looked like you could get tired just walking from the gate to the front door.

I wasn't so careless as to approach the residence. I'd noticed the security camera mounted on a gatepost. Naturally, there had to be other cameras. That was why I'd gotten out of the taxi well short of the place. Even now, I was still sixty feet or so away from the premises. There happened to be a van parked on the street, so I was hiding in its shadow.

Let me meet Katsutoshi Katsuragi, I thought. I'd see him in person and interrogate him. *What is it that you have against Shunsuke Sakuma? Exactly what part of my way of thinking is "superficial"? I didn't understand with just Kozuka's explanation. I can't begin to comprehend it.*

But looking at the giant, fort-like estate, I hesitated. If I visited at this time, there was no way Katsutoshi Katsuragi would even meet with me. I'd more likely be turned away at the gate. Announcing myself might be fruitless. They'd simply laugh that an unpleasantly stubborn ad man had come to complain. Even if I did meet him, right now my breath stank of alcohol. If Katsuragi thought I'd merely been driven by the momentum of being drunk, he'd no doubt immediately get up and walk away.

But it was true that I'd been driven by my inebriated state. When I told the taxi driver my destination, my head had been boiling over like a kettle on a stove.

There was nothing to it. In the end, when I was right in front of my enemy, I was chickening out. I was going wobbly. It was just that I was so scared of the humiliation of scramming and doing nothing that I couldn't leave it at that. Even listing all the reasons for not charging in was me making excuses to myself.

I grew more and more furious. My rage was directed at myself. *Shunsuke Sakuma, how could you be acting so small?*

I'd make a fresh start, I decided, my mind sobering. I wasn't running away. Without fail, I'd confront Katsutoshi Katsuragi. But the way I'd do it would have to be meticulous, just like me.

I pointed at the estate. Then I swore by my heart. *Just wait, Mr. Katsuragi. You'll learn my true strength, for sure.*

It happened then. Something in my peripheral vision moved. I looked toward the edge of the wall.

Someone was trying to scale it. Not trying to get in, but out. A human form stepped over the iron railing on the top and, after a reluctant pause, jumped down to the street. The figure fell on its backside but didn't seem hurt.

I thought it was a burglar for an instant, but that thought soon vanished. It was because I realized the person was a young woman. I'd never heard of a beskirted burglar.

The woman looked to be in her late teens, or in her early twenties at most. She was fairly beautiful, and her proportions weren't bad, either. She swiveled her head to examine her surroundings, so I hid in the van's shadow.

She started walking fast. After hesitating for a moment, I followed suit. When I passed by the front of the Katsuragi estate, I turned my head to the other side of the street to avoid the security camera.

It was on a hunch that I became interested in following her. I didn't think she'd broken into the Katsuragi residence. I thought it was more reasonable that she'd slipped out of the estate for some reason. So then what would that reason be? That was what I was interested in.

I saw no hint of her worrying about being shadowed. It was likely because I was keeping a good distance. When she got to a large road, she raised her hand and tried to hail a taxi. That was when I fretted. If she got in a cab, it'd be over.

I hurried out to the road. The taxi she had gotten in was leaving. Drilling the license-plate number into my brain, I waited for the next taxi to come. Luckily, a free car came by.

"Just head straight for now, as fast as possible," I said as I got in.

The driver didn't seem thrilled with the instructions and pulled out with a disgruntled look. I fluttered a ten-thousand-yen bill next to his face.

"There's a yellow taxi right in front of us. I want you to follow it."

"I don't want any trouble, mister."

"It's all right. There's a girl in that taxi, and I was asked by her parents to follow her."

"Huh."

The driver stepped on the accelerator. It seemed that was the conclusion of our negotiation. I placed the ten-thousand-yen bill on the small money tray.

I thought it'd be bad if we didn't catch up before we got to Kanpachi Avenue, but luckily, her taxi was stopped in front of a traffic light beforehand. I rechecked the number and told the driver, "It's that car."

"Why follow her? Are you trying to catch her?" the driver asked.

"No, I just need to figure out her destination."

"Ah, and you're reporting it to her parents?"

"Well, something like that."

"I see. She must be very precious."

I wasn't sure what his interpretation was, but it seemed the driver had drawn his own conclusion.

The taxi the girl was riding went south down Kanpachi Avenue. Mine did, too. Hers was not going particularly fast, so it wasn't especially hard to follow.

"I thought a young woman would head to Shibuya, but that doesn't seem to be the case, does it?" the driver said. Probably because we were heading in the exact opposite direction of Shibuya.

At that point, the taxi in front of us turned left. It was Nakahara Road.

"If we go straight, this takes us to Gotanda, right?" I asked.

"That's right. Recently, they say there are a lot of places to go out around Gotanda too."

Had she bothered to sneak out over their wall just to hit some bar? If she said she was going out at this hour, her parents certainly wouldn't take it with a smile. But her own face when she'd made her escape didn't seem like that of a young woman looking forward to a night out. There was something more urgent in her expression. I was following her like this because of that.

Gotanda station came into view. The taxi ahead of us showed no sign at all that it was stopping. It passed the station and this time turned right.

"Whoa, now it's Shinagawa," the driver said.

"That's what it seems like."

The girl's taxi entered Route One between Tokyo and Yokohama. We, too, continued on it. After a minute, I caught sight of the Japan Railways Shinagawa Station on the right side. The left side was lined with famous hotels.

"Ah, they're going to the left," the driver said. Certainly, the car in front of us had its blinker on.

"Follow them please."

"But we'll go into the hotel."

"I don't mind."

The hotel entrance was at the top of a gentle slope. The car in front of us stopped there. I also instructed the driver to stop, just below.

"I wonder if she might be meeting with some guy," the driver said as he issued the receipt.

That might be it, I humored him with a reply.

The girl went through the revolving doors and headed inside. After waiting a bit, I continued after her.

The driver's speculation might have been right. I could understand why she would sneak out of the estate in that manner if she were meeting a man secretly. But in that case, was I an awful clown to have tracked her all the way to this place? No, no, whatever it was, I would be at no disadvantage knowing the Katsuragis' secrets. My interest revived.

Going in, the front desk was to the left. No one was at the long counter now. The girl was ringing the call bell on top of the counter. Before long, a hotelkeeper wearing a gray uniform came from the back.

I pulled a ten-thousand-yen bill from my wallet and approached the girl from behind.

"I sincerely apologize, but tonight we're completely full," the hotelkeeper was telling the girl. It seemed she was trying to get a last-minute room.

"It doesn't matter what kind," the girl said. Her tone was listless.

She had the type of voice that you'd want to sing R&B.

"I'm sorry, but they're all occupied." The middle-aged hotelkeeper lowered his head respectfully, even to such a young lady. Then he turned his eyes towards me. "How may I help you?"

"I want 2000-yen bills. Could you break this for me? I just need five."

"For ten thousand yen? Please wait a moment."

The hotelkeeper momentarily withdrew to the back.

Without taking notice of me and with an aimless gait, the girl headed to the front entrance. I couldn't lose sight of her here. I left the counter. At that moment, a voice called from behind me, "Oh, sir."

"Thank you, it's okay."

I left the dumbfounded hotelkeeper behind and also headed outside.

The girl was just about to enter a pathway that crossed the hotel garden. Fearing that I would be suspected, I put some distance between us and tailed her. There were no signs she'd noticed me.

The pathway ended at the edge of the hotel's premises. Across the street was another hotel. I inferred what she intended to do.

Just as I thought, the girl went into the neighboring hotel. This one's front desk was on the first floor; it was always manned even in the middle of the night because businesspeople favored the place. I found a spot where I could observe the front desk and from there watched her actions.

The girl, who had been speaking with the hotelkeeper, abruptly pivoted and started walking. The result of their exchange was obvious from her sulking visage.

She went into a room with public phones. *I see*, I thought, and moved closer.

There she was in the middle of frantically flipping through the phone book. I knew which section she had turned to without even looking.

"At this time and with that appearance, it's impossible no matter which hotel you go to."

She jumped at my voice and looked at me with a surprised expression.

"A lone young woman with no reservation asking for a room just makes them suspicious. From the hotel's perspective, taking on a guest who isn't even paying them that much isn't worth the trouble they might get into."

It seemed she thought a creepy man had approached her with clear ulterior motives. She closed the phone book and tried to leave.

"You're trying to find lodgings for tonight, aren't you, Miss Katsuragi?"

Her feet stopped flat. Her neck turned around like a mechanized doll with noisy gears. "Who are you?"

I pulled a business card from my pocket. She alternated between looking at me and the printed characters.

"Cyberplan..."

"Advertising, producing, brokering, we do anything. Handymen for our corporate partners, as it were. Your company, Miss Katsuragi, is our greatest client. Well, since that's it for my self-introduction, I'd be pleased to get yours."

"I'm under no obligation." She flicked the business card with her fingertips. It fluttered to the floor.

"Then I'll have to fulfill mine." I picked up the card. "I can't overlook a thief who snuck into an important client's home."

The girl opened wide her slightly slanted eyes. She looked rather strong-headed, but also prettier that way. I continued looking into those eyes.

"Or else, it wasn't that you were sneaking in, but that you snuck out. Either way, I can't overlook it. I better contact Mr. Katsuragi." I pulled my cellphone out of my pocket.

"Stop."

"Then introduce yourself." I flashed her a smile. "Tell me what's going on, because I can be a fairly understanding guy. Depending on the situation, I might even be of assistance in getting you lodged for the night."

A hesitant look appeared on her face. No, perhaps it was a calculating look. She was making a guess as to my identity and wondering whether I could be trusted, whether she should get some use out of me.

She brought out her right hand. "That business card, please."

"As you wish."

Taking the card, she stuck out her left hand next. "Your license."

"My license?"

"Because this card might not be yours."

"Ah, I see."

Seeing her up close, she was younger than I'd thought. She might have been around high school age but was levelheaded. I pulled my license from my wallet. She used the ballpoint pen and memo pad set out next to the phone to take down my address.

"You're very careful," I said, putting away my license after she'd given it back to me.

"Papa says to always introduce myself at the very last moment."

"Papa?"

"Katsutoshi Katsuragi."

"Ah," I nodded. "Of course. But why in the world would the daughter of Nissei Automobile's executive vice president scale their wall and break out?"

"That doesn't have anything to do with you, does it?"

"Well, it's true I have nothing to do with it, but the reality is that I've met you. If something happened to you afterwards, I'd be brought to account. My company might not survive that."

"Why should I care?"

She tried to leave, so I pulled out my cellphone again. "I'm going to call. Right now."

She turned around with a fed-up face. "I'm saying you can leave me alone, isn't that good enough for you? Can't you listen to the orders of the executive vice president's daughter?"

"Unfortunately, it's the EVP who's important to me, not his daughter per se." I pretended to press the buttons on my cellphone.

"Stop it."

She tried to snatch it. I evaded her.

Right then, a middle-aged guy who looked to be a businessman came by. He watched us dubiously.

"You don't want to draw people's attention in this place, right?" I said. "Would you talk with me somewhere else?"

She thought it over again. I should say she started calculating again. After a while she nodded.

We went to a café next to the hotel. That's to say, a self-service venue where you had to bring your drink to your own seat. We headed over to a counter facing the street and sat side by side.

I had thought of two ways I could make use of her. One was that I could somehow take her back to the Katsuragi estate tonight. It would mean I'd have a huge advantage over Katsutoshi Katsuragi. If I became the guy who protected his precious daughter, any man would have to change his tune.

The other way was by listening to her story. There was no mistaking that since she had snuck out of the estate, she held some sort of secret. It would also be the Katsuragi family's secret. When I confronted Katsutoshi Katsuragi after this, that would also probably serve as a great weapon.

After taking a sip of her coffee, she broke the silence. "How long have you been watching me?"

"From the mansion. I saw you when you went over the wall."

"Why were you in front of my house?"

"The reason wasn't important. I was nearby because of work so I thought I'd gawk at the famous Katsuragi residence."

"I thought no one was in the street."

"I was a little ways away. If I looked at the house from up close, I'd get caught by the security camera, wouldn't I?"

"Well, after that, you followed me? Why? For what?"

"I feel like I'm getting interrogated by a detective." I grinned wryly and sipped my coffee. "I told you earlier. Mr. Katsuragi is a very important man to us. It'd be natural for us to go investigate if we saw someone climb over the wall and leave his estate, wouldn't it?"

"Why didn't you talk to me immediately?"

"Is that what you wanted?"

When I asked, she sank into silence. I took another sip of my coffee.

"I thought maybe there was some sort of reason, so I thought I'd watch you for a bit. But I didn't think I'd end up following you all the way here."

"Strange taste."

"If I weren't like that for my work, I wouldn't be any good. Now I get to ask some questions. First, introduce yourself."

"I already did."

"All I've heard is that you're the EVP's daughter. I'd like to know your name. I need something to call you, don't I?"

She watched the street through the glass window, but eventually muttered, "Juri."

"What?"

"Juri. As in the first characters from 'arbor' and 'science.'"

"Ah, so it's Miss Juri. Juri Katsuragi. Indeed, just hearing your name, I know you're no pleb."

"What do you mean?"

"I'm praising you. Anyway, I'm wondering what circumstances

in the world would make Miss Juri Katsuragi climb over her own house's wall?"

She sighed at my question. Her slender shoulders rose and fell. "Does that mean I have to tell you?"

"If you don't want to, you don't have to, but…" I reached my hand towards the pocket my cellphone was in.

"Fine. You're saying you're going to tell my parents, right?"

"It's what you call adult responsibility. Take your pick."

"Let me think a little." Juri rested her chin in her hands on the counter. She was surprisingly fair for girls nowadays. You could call her skin porcelain; its surface didn't even have a trace of unevenness. It wasn't just from being young. That took work.

As I gazed at her beautiful profile, she faced me abruptly. I pulled back in a flash.

"Could I get a refill on the coffee?" she asked.

"Sure thing."

As I cleared the empty cup, I took the opportunity to drink mine as well and bought two more cups of coffee. When I got back to the seats, Juri was smoking Caster Super Milds.

"I can't praise you for smoking while you're still young."

"Agreed. But if I were older, would you praise me?"

"I don't smoke."

"Because of your health?"

"More than that, I think it's a waste of time. If it takes about three minutes to smoke one cigarette, then people who smoke a whole pack a day waste one hour out of twenty-four just smoking. They might say they're actually working while they smoke, but that's bull. Another reason: in order to smoke, you have to sacrifice a hand. There's hardly any line of work that benefits from you using one hand instead of both."

Juri faced me and blew smoke into my face. "Is it any fun thinking that way?"

"It's not because it's fun, it's just that I don't like wasteful things. Anyway, have you come to a decision?"

Juri put out her cigarette in the ashtray with some care and brought her second cup of coffee to her mouth.

"To put it simply, I was running away from home."

"Running away?"

"That's right. I came to hate being in that house, so I ran away. That's why I can't get caught by my parents. That's why I had to climb over the wall."

"I don't buy it."

"Why not?"

"That's not something you do in such light gear." Her luggage was just one small handbag.

"You can believe it or not, but don't get in my way." She took a second cigarette out of the pack.

I sighed and looked around. I didn't want anyone to think I was trying to woo a young woman, but I had a mountain of stuff I wanted to get out of her.

"I got it," I conceded. "I'll accept that you were running away. But I can't let you escape from my sight just yet. I'd like to hear the reason why you're running. If I think it's not unreasonable for you to run away, I'll turn a blind eye tonight."

Juri blew smoke at me. "Why do I need your permission to run away?"

"Because that's the situation. I suppose you'll just have to resign yourself to the fact that you were unlucky enough to be witnessed. So tell me." I motioned with my right palm, leading her on.

Still holding the cigarette between her fingers, she bit the thumb nail on her other hand. Her nails and teeth were also well-maintained, beautiful.

After taking that thumb from her mouth, she side-eyed me.

"It was Mr. Sakuma, right?"

"I'm glad you remembered," I answered smugly.

"What I'm about to tell you—can you promise me you won't tell anyone?"

"I want to say I'll promise, but it'll depend on what you say."

"Hmph." She looked over at me again and stared fixedly. "You're pretty honest. I thought you'd say you'd promise."

"It'd be meaningless to make that promise." It was easy to say I'd promise, but she wasn't the type of girl to talk if I did.

"I guess there's no guarantee you'd honor your promise anyway."

"That's the way it is. But I can say this. My attitude depends on if I benefit from it. And if I'm not going to, I don't particularly want to be known as a gossipy guy. Especially not by a favored client's daughter."

The corner of Juri's lips twisted. I couldn't tell whether she thought I was being unpleasant.

She took several pulls from her cigarette in rapid succession. I decided to watch as she blew gray smoke incessantly.

"You know, I—" Juri started, "I'm not really a Katsuragi."

"Ah." I gazed at her profile. This had caught me flat-footed. "Is that right?"

"It might not be accurate to say 'not really.' Officially…yeah, I should say officially I'm not his daughter."

"Either way, it's still a surprising confession. If it's true."

"If you're not going to believe me, you can forget about it. Because I won't tell you any more."

"Hey, hey," I pleaded with a soothing gesture. "Don't think it's unreasonable for me to be surprised. I won't interrupt you again, so let me hear the rest."

Juri gave a light snort. Her expression betrayed disdain for a mere gossip-lover. Given the circumstances, I resigned myself to taking that look.

"Did you know Papa married a second time?"

"I've heard about that. But wasn't this almost twenty years ago?"

"Exactly twenty. He divorced his last wife with mutual consent. With his current wife, he has one daughter."

"It seems unlikely that that daughter is you."

She wouldn't call her own mother "his current wife." But she had also said "last wife." That suggested she wasn't the child of the last wife, either.

"I'm actually the child of his last lover."

She said it so plainly that I couldn't reply. I blinked with my mouth half-open.

"It might not be right to say that she was his last lover. She might have been his lover before last, or maybe even the one before. Anyway, that guy doesn't stop." She smiled with just her lips. Apparently by "that guy" she meant her father.

"Are you saying she's a lover from Mr. Katsuragi's earlier marriage?"

"Well, yeah. The divorce seemed to have something to do with it, too. Apparently, his last wife was a high-class lady from a good family, so even though she was dealing with the mighty Katsuragis, she must not have been able to stand it."

Listening to Juri's story, I couldn't help but chuckle. It was a fine joke that Katsutoshi Katsuragi had fumbled his private life.

"Then, why are you, the daughter of a lover, living with the Katsuragis?"

"It's simple. Because my mom died. Apparently it was leukemia. They say she was really beautiful, and also that beauties die young," Juri said without any note of sorrow.

"You don't remember your mom?"

"I feel like I remember her faintly, but..." She shook her head. "I don't really know. Maybe I don't remember. Maybe I've seen pictures and are mistaking them for memories."

A coolheaded analysis. "When did the Katsuragis take you in?"

"When I was eight. But my mom died when I was three. During that time, my grandmother took care of me."

At eight, her personality would have finished forming. I imagined how Juri must have felt being taken away, and felt some sympathy for her. "I wonder why Mr. Katsuragi didn't try to take you in until you were eight."

"Who knows. Maybe because of his new wife. His legit daughter had been born by then."

"In that case, I wonder why he decided to take you in."

"Because my grandmother fell ill. Someone had to raise me, huh? Papa did recognize me as his own, and he must've thought that taking me into his home as his daughter at that point was better than someone else doing it and raising hell."

Juri put out her cigarette in the ashtray.

"You've been at that house since then?"

"In a way."

"In a way?"

"Think about it. If you suddenly had someone else's kid come in, even if it's an eight year old, your new wife and real daughter wouldn't feel good about it. Even Papa knew that, so they sent me to a boarding school. Up north in Sendai, too."

"From elementary school?"

"From elementary school to high school. The only times I'd go home were during long vacations. But then, I didn't feel like going home one bit. I wanted to stay in the dormitories forever. But according to the school rules, unless there were special circumstances, you had to go home. I hated summer vacation and even winter vacation and spring vacation. I thought if we just didn't have those things I'd be all set. Normal kids get excited when vacation gets closer and lament that it's over, but I was completely the opposite. How I awaited the end of August."

Juri was looking at the street through the glass. It was an expression that housed both loneliness and emptiness. She might have gone through her childhood with that face.

"Are you a college student?"

"Yeah. Sophomore."

I thought of asking her at which school, but didn't. It was irrelevant, and there were other things I wanted to ask her about more. "So that's how you came back to Tokyo."

"I really wanted to stay in Sendai. It didn't even have to be Sendai, I wanted to attend a college outside of Tokyo. But when they told me to come back, I had no choice. Because they've been taking care of me."

"Mr. Katsuragi told you to come?"

"Yeah. Well, I know what Papa was thinking, basically."

"What do you mean?"

"To put it simply, he started worrying about the future. He wants to hurry and marry me off to someone. To do that, he needs to keep me close, right?"

"I see." It was strange enough, but I understood. "So, unable to bear your current life, you ran away. Climbing over that wall."

"You get it now?"

"I grasp the circumstances. But did you really hate it that much? You didn't get along with everyone at home?"

"I can't say I didn't." She tried to take out another cigarette, but it seemed her previous one had been the last. She crushed the empty box in her hand. "This isn't 'Cinderella,' and it's not like I was bullied. But I've experienced plenty of invisible malice. In the end, I wasn't really family. No matter how many years passed, I couldn't blend in. For their part, they never accepted me. If I weren't there, they'd be a perfect family. When I'm there, it's like I'm an actress in a soap opera. Everything I say and do is fake, and it's so suffocating." She looked at me. "Do you see?"

"Somehow," I answered. "What about you? Are your feelings about the Katsuragis all negative? Regarding your new mother, for instance?"

"That's a mean question." She took a long breath. "You think I could come to like them? People who kept ignoring me? Smiling all the while. With smiling masks."

Well put, I admired. "What about the daughter? Um, I guess I should say your half-sister."

"Oh, her." Juri closed her mouth and inclined her head. Her face said she was choosing her words. Still wearing that expression she answered, "I hate her."

3

When I checked into the Kayabacho Polar Hotel, it was past midnight. It was a business hotel that acquaintances of mine patronized when they came to Tokyo, so if I showed my face at the front desk, they'd be accommodating. Tonight I had Juri wait behind the stairs and went through the procedures.

"Well, I don't have any intention of being complicit with you running away from home, but you trusted me and told me a lot of stuff, so I'll treat you."

After getting into the room, I put the key on top of the tiny desk. The room only had a small single bed, a TV, the desk, and a refrigerator.

"For the time being, I've rented it out for two nights. Checkout is the day after tomorrow at noon." Saying so, I glanced at the clock. "It's already past midnight, so I should say tomorrow," I corrected myself.

"Why for two nights?"

"Just in case. Sleep well for tonight, and then if you feel like going home, go whenever you like. But when you do, give me a ring."

"What you mean is, if I'm not going home, I should stay put."

"It's late, so for now just sleep well. Let's talk again tomorrow." I started heading to the door, but stopped and turned around. "Um, you have money, right?"

She looked away at that. Her eyelashes fluttered.

"You tried to stay in a hotel without any?"

"I have a card."

"Hah, a family card." I pulled out two ten-thousand-yen bills from my wallet. "Anyway, I'll leave this. In case of an emergency."

"I don't need it."

"Then you can just leave it here." I put the ten-thousand-yen bills on top of the TV and put the remote on it as a paperweight. "See you tomorrow. I'll pray you'll come to your senses. Let me tell you, as soon as a family card is reported you won't be able to use it. Without money, just what are you thinking of doing?"

Not waiting for Juri's reply, I did head to the door this time. When I turned the knob, she spoke to me from behind.

"I should have helped myself."

At her one liner, I turned around again. "What was that?"

"I ought to have grabbed some money. If not cash, then something valuable. A diamond or whatever. Then I wouldn't have had to worry for a while."

"Goes to show how impulsive you were. Tomorrow you'll change your mind. Anyway, for now, I'm not contacting Mr. Katsuragi."

"I won't ever go back home."

"Well, take your time thinking it over."

"I have a little bit of a claim to that household's fortune, don't I?"

I was taken aback for a moment by her off-kilter question. I shrugged. "Probably. But you'd need to keep being their daughter."

"You mean if I leave, then I wouldn't?"

"Who knows. But thinking about that now is meaningless. You wouldn't inherit anything until Mr. Katsuragi passes away. That's decades in the future."

"I heard there's a way to before anyone dies."

"You mean an advance? It's not impossible, but that would be for Mr. Katsuragi to decide. I don't know about you demanding one.

Either way, you'd have to go home first."

She'd realized she was penniless and was remembering only now the enormity of what she was losing. That she'd worry about her fortune as a runaway had to be Katsutoshi Katsuragi's blood in her.

I turned the doorknob. "Well, goodnight."

"Wait a second."

I turned around with the door still slightly ajar. "What now?"

"Could I ask you for a favor?" She pulled her chin in and looked up at me. It was a face she hadn't shown until now.

"Depends on what it is."

"It's nothing difficult. First, call home and just tell them I'm with you."

"That's all you want?"

"After that, I want you to go get money. Tell them that I'm not going home and that I need enough money to live off of."

I shut the door. If anyone heard this, it could spell trouble. Then, studying Juri's face to make sure she wasn't kidding, I spread my arms and said, "Are you serious? Or are you pulling my leg?"

"If I called, they'd just tell me to come home."

"It'd be the same if I called. They'd tell me to hurry up and bring their daughter home if I had the time to be making a stupid call. I told you earlier, but Mr. Katsuragi is an important client of ours. Even setting you up here is an act of betrayal."

"You could just say that I don't want to go home."

"Like that would convince him. In the worst case, I'd end up being accused of kidnapping you."

"Then how about you say it's a kidnapping?"

"Huh?"

"Without introducing yourself, just say: *If you want your daughter back, prepare ten million yen in cash.*"

I squatted and peered at her face from below. "Are you sane?"

"I'm not going home, okay, and I need money. I'm ready to do anything."

"I think I see." I threw up my arms halfway, nodding. "Might I recommend a cold shower? It seems like this has gotten you all fired up."

It seemed like Juri still wanted to say something, but I ignored her and left the room.

The hotel was a ten-minute walk from my condo. Turning over my conversation with Juri in my mind, I walked down the nighttime streets. I'd had quite a bit to drink since early in the evening, but I wasn't feeling the least bit intoxicated. Talking with her had been just that stimulating.

Katsutoshi Katsuragi's household being so troubled was a surprise. I was undecided on how I might use the fact, but knowing about it didn't hurt. There might come a time when it would serve as a trump card. The funk I'd been in only several hours ago had vanished without a trace.

The next day when I arrived at work, Kozuka called me in. When I went to his office, he was right in the middle of talking to Tomoya Sugimoto. Sugimoto generally did work that had to do with concerts and anything related to music. He was a year younger than me, but accomplished in his own way. I recalled that he would be my replacement for the Nissei Automobile job.

"I was just in the middle of telling Sugimoto about yesterday's matter," Kozuka said, looking at me.

Sugimoto must have felt awkward meeting my eyes and dropped his gaze to the surface of the president's desk.

"Are you telling me to debrief him on the job?"

"No, there's no need for that. We need to start over from scratch anyway. If we don't, our partners won't consent." He meant Katsutoshi Katsuragi wouldn't. "Did you already tell the staff about how the automobile park was canceled?"

"No, I was just about to."

"Right." Kozuka looked like he was in thought.

"Was there anything else?"

"Yes. Actually, I've been thinking a lot since then, but it's still going to be hard to remake a new team from scratch now. I might change part of it, but swapping out the whole crew is physically impossible, isn't it?"

I realized what he wanted to say. "You're saying that you're going to leave the team as is. And just swapping out the team leader."

"Well, that's how it is. Anyway, we don't have time. Nissei also consented to that."

How convenient. I swallowed my words and nodded.

"Also, I have a meeting with Nissei this afternoon. I want you to attend."

"Me? What for?" I'd donned a forced smile. "I thought I was useless to them."

"Don't whine. They want to explain it properly from their end. You can leave after Sugimoto's introduction."

They were saying the prior supervisor should attend the announcement of the new supervisor. I couldn't recall ever being humiliated as badly as that.

Juri's face suddenly floated into my mind. That's when I thought of something.

"Mr. Katsuragi won't come anyway, right?"

"No, you'll probably see him."

"Are you sure?" I tilted my head to the side. "I don't think he'll be able to attend."

"Why are you saying this? I just got confirmation. The person clearly said that Executive Vice President Katsuragi would be there."

"Just now?"

"That's right. Is there something the matter with that?"

"No..."

Did he have the composure to sit in a meeting when his daughter had run away from home? Or did Katsutoshi Katsuragi not know that Juri had gone missing? That was hard to believe. If anyone noticed, they'd tell her father right away.

"I understand. I'll attend. I'll take a *very* thorough look at Mr. Katsuragi's face."

"Don't you make any trouble. All you have to do is be quiet until it's over," Kozuka warned, pointing at my chest.

Nissei Automobile's Tokyo headquarters were in Shinjuku. After going through a few overblown formalities, we were led to the conference room. They were already waiting.

We received the gist of the explanation about redoing the plan from their fat promotions manager. It was gentler than what Kozuka had said yesterday, but it was the same difference in that they'd knocked my ideas.

Katsutoshi Katsuragi wasn't there. They said he was late, but he probably wouldn't come. There was no way he could come. He might have been filing a missing person report with the police right around then.

The promotions manager shifted to how they would proceed. Concept, needs, IT—he threw out words that decent ad men would be ashamed to string together. I became bored. Sugimoto's introduction was over, so I'd leave when the timing was right.

It happened after I'd already bitten down on several yawns. Without a knock, the door opened. A broad-shouldered man wearing a dark suit came in. The promotions manager broke off.

After surveying the room with keen eyes, the man went to the head of the table.

There was no mistaking he was Katsutoshi Katsuragi.

"What, why did you stop?" He threw a dissatisfied look at the promotions manager.

The manager tried to hurry and resume, but apparently having forgotten where he was, he just looked flustered for a moment. In other words, he was that intimidated.

"Is that Mr. Katsuragi?" I asked Kozuka, who was next to me, in a whisper. Kozuka just nodded slightly with his chin.

The promotions manager eventually got back his rhythm and reprised his tedious lecturing. Not bothering to listen, I stared, out of the corners of my eyes, at the face of the EVP who had casually dissed my abilities. Katsutoshi Katsuragi also seemed uninterested in what the manager had to say. I couldn't tell if it was because the fellow wasn't saying much, or for some other reason—namely, that his daughter was missing.

The manager finished, and when another person from the Nissei Automobile side tried to stand up next, Katsuragi raised his hand, saying, *Hold it*. As everyone watched, he opened his mouth without standing up.

"We're aware that we're troubling you through this upcoming project change. However, please understand that we aren't here to host some festival. We do require innovation, but I don't intend to gamble with luck. The name of the game we're playing here is none other than business. It requires scrupulous planning and bold action. Since it's a game, we're playing to win. We can't treat it as a joke just because it's a game. In this world, games where you have to put everything on the line are as numerous as the stars. Please, think of this one as such. And I'm fairly confident when it comes to games. Being confident, I've concluded that our game plan needs overhauling—that's our situation."

He had just about said that we were pawns that needed to move however he wished. No, that was all he wanted to say. Although his tone was calm and gentle, his voice was equipped with a force that resonated across the room. I felt everyone's postures stiffen compared to a few minutes ago.

I ended up sitting in until the end. In that time, I continued to secretly observe Katsutoshi Katsuragi, but I sensed nothing absent-minded about him. When his subordinates or Kozuka spoke, the man's expression looked incurious at first glance, but the sharp light in the back of his eyes never dwindled. *Well, he's certainly not just anybody,* I admitted.

My sense of humiliation and fighting spirit mixed and swirled as though they'd been put in a blender. A game? That served me just fine. So he styled himself a master? But when it came to games, I was no slouch, either. We could decide who was the true master. He was going to send me packing and not even play me? *Katsutoshi Katsuragi, take me on,* I kept willing at him. But he didn't seem to receive the signal.

After the meeting, Kozuka rushed over to Katsuragi's side, greeted him, and tried to introduce me. But without even looking in my direction, Katsuragi cheerlessly waved his hand and turned his back to us.

"We'll skip the superfluous stuff. No point in my meeting an outsider to all this."

With those words, he immediately started walking away.

Speechless, Kozuka and I watched the major-corporation EVP's back. I could almost sense the looks of pity that the others present were casting at me.

As I gritted my teeth to bear my humiliation, Kozuka patted my shoulder twice.

That evening, I was dining with a woman named Maki at an Italian restaurant in Akasaka. Maki was an aspiring model. But she'd probably only done a few real modeling jobs. The types of gigs that came to her were things like being a campaign girl or an event companion. I was also aware she worked at a hostess club a few nights a week to pay her bills. Up until now, I'd never invited her out myself. The one who called was always her. I wasn't stupid enough to think she'd fallen in love with me. I was probably just an important connection to her.

But tonight I was the one who'd called. I didn't feel like going home without blowing a little steam first. After dinner, we'd go drinking somewhere, and depending on the flow of the conversation, I might try to get her into bed. Having a physical relationship could cause some hassles down along the line, but I thought it was better than spending the night with my own emotions.

By the time our fish came out, one bottle of white wine had been emptied. I ordered the same thing. If a meat dish came out, I could also order red wine then.

"Aren't you fast," Maki said as she clumsily brought her food to her mouth. She was on a diet and consciously over-chewed. I was a little annoyed, but I couldn't ruin the mood.

"Maybe it's because I'm feeling high. And when I get nervous, I get thirsty." I tilted my glass.

"Why are you feeling high?"

"It's because you met with me. I invited you suddenly, so I was sure you'd refuse."

"Don't say that. You're such a sweet talker." She pretended to laugh it off, but her eyes said that she didn't mind one bit.

"When I'm just straightforward, I'm not taken seriously. It's really hard to praise a woman in Japan. But I'm really nervous. It's a bit of a mystery to me, too."

Huh, she tilted her head.

"First off, meeting a woman face to face like this over a meal is something I haven't done in a while. Another thing, up until now I hadn't ever contacted you. I wonder if it's from the guilt of breaking that commandment."

"Now that you mention it, you're right. Why today? Was it on some whim?"

"I don't blame you for thinking so, the way I invited you, but I'd tried a number of times. But no matter what I couldn't make the call.

But then tonight, I suddenly found the courage."

Mere white lies.

"Did something happen at work?" Maki peered into my face.

"No, not really." I lifted my glass. I wasn't in the mood to tell her in detail about my affairs. That wasn't the role she served.

Packing the passable meal and wine into my stomach, I offered information I thought Maki would find interesting and presented related anecdotes, interspersing light jokes in between. I was fully aware that a young woman wouldn't feel satisfied just hearing her partner hold forth, so after that I switched over to listening. Her talk was juvenile, worked up to nothing, and moreover hadn't a hint of structure, so I could barely keep from falling asleep at how boring it was. Still, biting down on my yawns, I nodded along like I'd never heard anything so captivating before. She probably thought that just for tonight she'd become an able conversationalist.

It was like a game between men and women, too, after all. But if your opponent wasn't good, the game wasn't any fun. On that note, tonight's playmate left me wanting. Looking at Maki's happy face, I wondered if I should have invited out the other woman. Being an office lady, she'd probably have been on guard about a sudden invitation, and I'd have had to make full use of various techniques to make it work. What to talk about at the table would have posed a challenge as well. But if you were going to date a woman, it was better when you had to focus a little.

In short, what I sought from women wasn't their bodies but a stimulating, sophisticated game. Sex was nothing but a reward for victory.

It wasn't just romance, I was like that about everything. I saw it all as a game, and victory granted me joy. Sports, of course, but my studies, too, I'd approached that way. Good or bad test scores meant nothing but winning or losing. College entrance exams were the epitome of that. If I earned a big run there, victory in the ultimate game, life, would be in my hands. I faced my entrance exams with that belief and successfully got into the college of my choice. Even in the job market, I did everything conceivable and got into the company I wanted. I thanked my planning for everything.

In my life so far, I hadn't lost a whole lot of matches. Even without Katsutoshi Katsuragi telling me, work was indeed a game for me. Nissei Automobile's campaign, too. And I had believed that the automobile park plan was certain to wrest victory, and still did now.

He was fairly confident when it came to games?

Then we had to play. We had to find out once and for all who the true master was.

But what could I do? My opponent had robbed me of my chance to fight. Sadly, there was no way for me to challenge him to a match.

"What's wrong?" Maki looked at me, puzzled. I had been in thought and missed her story, it seemed.

"No, nothing. I think I've had too much wine." I smiled and scooped a mouthful of my sherbet dessert.

After leaving the restaurant, I tried asking her if she wanted to drink some more. Without hesitating one bit, Maki consented. I hailed a cab.

"But I feel relieved. Because you seem to be doing fine," Maki said after the taxi started moving.

"What do you mean?"

"Well, because..." After pausing and choosing her words, she opened her mouth again. "I was worried you were depressed. Or if you weren't depressed, that you were in a bad mood..."

"Well, that's weird. Why would I be depressed or in a bad mood?"

At that, she looked at me awkwardly with upturned eyes. "During the day today, I talked with Jun over the phone. You know her, right? Jun Ueno?"

"Of course I do." Junko Ueno was an employee of Cyberplan.

She was also the reason I had come to know Maki. Apparently they had been friends since high school. "Did she say something?"

"Yeah, she mentioned you and said that you were probably blue."

"Blue?"

"She said you'd been given an important project but suddenly been let off of it…"

"She said that?"

"Yeah."

I sighed. Undoubtedly every single employee in the whole company knew that Shunsuke Sakuma had been removed from the Nissei Automobile campaign, and all kinds of rumors were circulating. Among those employees were probably some who were gratified. People whose work I had disparaged or who thought I'd gotten the better of them weren't hard to find.

"Jun said that letting you off was stupid. That there wasn't anyone as perfect as you."

"I'm honored she'd go so far as to say that." Having someone like Junko Ueno say stuff like that didn't make me happy at all. In fact, being pitied by her was humiliating.

"I'm not lying. Other than at crime, she said no one could beat you."

"Huh…"

That caught unexpectedly at something in my heart. I had a feeling like you do just before realizing you'd forgotten some item. Eventually, it took on a clear shape and floated into my mind as an idea.

"Excuse me, please stop here," I told the driver. "One person will get off here."

Next to me Maki's eyes widened. "What's wrong?"

"Sorry. I remembered something urgent. I'll make up for this."

I took two ten-thousand-yen bills out of my wallet, forced them on her, and got out. Maki looked dumbstruck as she watched me from the taxi that had started moving again.

I hailed a replacement. As I got in I said, "To Kayabacho."

I got off in front of Kayabacho Polar Hotel and went through the entrance. Bypassing the front desk, I headed to the elevator hall.

When I knocked on the room door, I got no answer from inside. I tried knocking again. Still no response. Just as I was wondering if she'd dared to check out without my consent, the door opened. From a small gap, Juri showed her face.

"Hi," I said.

"You're alone, right?"

"Yup."

She nodded and closed the door, undid the chain, then finally opened the door again.

When I went in, the TV was on. It was a program introducing the current top songs. It seemed Juri had been lying on bed watching it. Snacks that she must have been working through were spread on the bed. On top of the nightstand were an ashtray and a bottle of juice.

"Have you eaten anything proper?"

"I just went to a family restaurant."

"And the menu?"

"Do you need to pry that much?"

"I'm worried about your health. I need you to be eating nutritious meals."

"Huh." Looking at my face, she took a seat on the bed. "Because if you brought a valued customer's daughter back home and she were emaciated, you'd give a bad impression?"

The girl was as obnoxious as ever. It made me want to put her in her place.

I drew a chair and sat down on it. I took the remote and turned off the TV.

"And? Do you feel like going home now?"

"I told you I wouldn't. Get off my back."

"I need to make sure. Because it's important."

"It's important?" She scowled. "How?"

"I'll explain later. I want to check one more thing. Last night, you told me you wanted me to get you money. Whatever amount you'd rightfully inherit, you even said. Was that a joke?"

"Why would I ever joke about that? I'm not a kid, it's not like I ran away to see how much my parents care about me."

"So you're really serious." I glared at her.

"I'm telling you I am. How many times are you going to make me say it?" she told me irritatedly.

"Splendid."

Still in the chair, I opened the fridge next to me. I took out a can of Budweiser and popped the top. The fizz vigorously overflowed down my fingers.

I had a mouthful and put the can on the desk. I examined Juri's expression anew. She stared back at me dubiously, looking a little creeped out.

It was time for me to decide. Hearing my proposal, how would this girl react? If she turned me down, it'd be game over at that moment. She'd simply tell her father just how crazy in the head Shunsuke Sakuma was. Without a doubt, her father would tell Kozuka and demand that I be fired immediately. Kozuka could never go against Katsutoshi Katsuragi. I would be driven out of the company.

But clinging to Cyberplan as things stood would just make me miserable. In that case, I wanted a match.

I was remembering the arcade games I played as a kid. After Space Invaders went out of style, countless others appeared. When a new one came out, I would go by the arcade. Backed by colorful images, the machine would propose a duel.

INSERT COIN—it was the same as then.

I opened my mouth at last. "How about a game?"

"A game?" Juri looked suspicious.

"A game that'll grant your wish. You'll be able to snatch from the Katsuragis whatever you're worth. I get compensated, too."

"What are you up to?"

"Asks who? This was your idea in the first place." I took the can of beer in hand again. Gulping it down, I fixed her with a gaze and continued, "A kidnapping game."

4

When she entered the condo unit, before taking off her shoes, Juri's nose twitched.

"Do you smell something?" I asked.

"No. I thought it'd smell more like a man. But it smells pretty good. Is it mint?"

"It's just the deodorant. I don't like the room to smell, either. Even if it's my own smell."

My place was a one bedroom. Juri sat down on the loveseat in the living room. She looked around and said, "So you keep it pretty clean."

"I clean it up once a week."

"Huh, you don't look like you would."

"If you make a habit out of it, it's nothing. The important thing is to make sure that you don't collect too much stuff. I keep throwing out all the extra stuff. If you do that, cleaning up isn't hard at all. As long as you have thirty minutes, you can get it done. One week is ten thousand eighty minutes, so if you just put in some effort for thirty minutes, you can spend about ten thousand minutes in comfort. But if you don't put in the thirty minutes of effort, you'll have to spend ten thousand minutes in discomfort."

As she listened to me, Juri made a blatantly disgusted face. "Do you have anything to drink?" she asked.

"Should I put on a pot of coffee?"

She didn't nod. She had her eyes on a Swedish board placed on the wall. "Some liquor would be nice."

She was such a cheeky girl. But tonight I'd humor her. "Okay. Beer, scotch, bourbon, brandy, sake," I listed, putting up my fingers. "What do you want?"

Juri crossed her legs, then her arms. "I want Dom Pérignon. Pink."

Did she want me to slap her? But I held back. "Usually I have two or three refrigerated, but last night I happened to drink my last one. I do have wine, though, if you'll pardon me."

Juri sighed, or rather, huffed, "It can't be helped, I guess. Make it red then."

She must have been trying to come across as an adult woman. Well, I'd put her in a good mood. "Understood, mademoiselle."

I had Italian wine that I'd received as a gift lying in the corner of my cupboard. I used a screw-type opener to pull the cork.

Tilting her glass, Juri took some time mouthing the wine. I predicted she'd say it was a little young or something like that.

But she nodded as though satisfied. "Yeah, it's good."

"Glad to hear it. Are you selective about your wine?"

"Not really," she denied unceremoniously. "If I drink it and I think it tastes good, that's good enough. Remembering the maker is too much work."

"But you know Dom Pérignon."

"It's the only champagne I know. My dad likes to say, 'Dom Pérignon equals champagne, and anything else is a different drink.'"

Katsutoshi Katsuragi's face wandered into my mind. I had to object. "Champagne just means a fizzy wine made in the Champagne region. But it's not just Dom Pérignon."

Juri shook her head at this. "Actually, how to make champagne was a secret process handed down at the Hautvillers monastery in Champagne. Then it spread to the entire region. The person who invented that process was the cellar master of the monastery, Dom Pérignon. That's why Dom Pérignon is the true champagne."

"Well, well." I knocked back my cheap red wine. "That was illuminating."

It was revolting. Katsutoshi Katsuragi probably spouted wisdom like that tilting his champagne flute.

"Anyway, I want to continue on with what we talked about earlier," I said.

"About the game?" As expected, Juri's expression became tense.

"Of course. I want to check one more time that you're serious about doing this."

"If I weren't I wouldn't have come here."

"Give it to me straight. Are you feeling up to a kidnapping game or not? If you're hesitating, tell me. Depending on the case, I'll give you time to think."

But at my words, she shook her head as though annoyed. "I told you I didn't run away from home as a joke, didn't I? I even have a grudge against the Katsuragis. I'm in."

"All right. Then how about a toast before we begin." I refilled our wine glasses and lifted mine. "May victory be ours."

Juri also hoisted her glass and clinked it against mine.

It wasn't as though I had an amazing strategy. Everything was still up in the air at this stage. But, for the first time in a while, I was excited. It was my response to coming across a game that was worth the challenge.

"There are two or three things I need to check." I put up my index finger. "First, after you left home, did you talk to anyone? For instance, did you call any friends?"

Juri immediately shook her head. "There's no way I'd do that. I'd be in trouble if they told on me."

"Right. Then next, go over what you've been doing from yesterday to today. Uhh, you said you went to a family restaurant. Which one?"

"Why do you need to dig so deep?"

"Because I want to know who you've come into contact with. If, by some chance, someone remembered your face, that would be a hassle."

"That won't be a problem."

"Listen. Why do you think criminals get caught by the police? Because they're all careless about their actions. You need to be conscious of where you left what traces, otherwise you can't anticipate the police's movements."

"But do you think the waitress at the restaurant would remember me? She meets tons of guests day in and day out. There were dozens even when I went. I bet she doesn't take a decent look at the guests' faces."

"I'd love to think so. But we need to be aware that your face was seen."

Juri sighed. "It's the Denny's when you go out of the hotel and go straight right. While I'm at it, I had shrimp doria, a salad, and coffee."

I took the notepad and pen from the phone stand and jotted down: Denny's, shrimp doria, salad, coffee. "Did you sit at the counter?"

"I took a window table. The smoking area wasn't as crowded."

"You didn't do anything that'd make an impression on anyone there?"

"Not that I know of."

"Was any guest staring at you?"

"Why would anyone?"

"You're pretty beautiful, so some guy might have wanted to hit on you," I replied, looking at Juri's well-proportioned features.

Without even smiling, she turned her face away. "There may have been, but I didn't notice anyone. I try to make as little eye contact as I can in those kinds of places anyway."

"Appropriately," I commended her. "What about after you left the restaurant?"

"I went to a convenience store and bought snacks and juice." She must have meant the fare that had been scattered over the bed.

"Where?"

"Across from the restaurant."

I knew that store well. It sold alcohol, so I'd been there to buy a beer in the middle of the night. "You just bought snacks and juice, right? You didn't chat with any employee?"

"He was an older guy who looked like he'd just been laid off. He had his hands full just trying not to mess up at the register."

"So you just went home after the convenience store." Seeing her nod, I continued, "Did any of the people in the hotel see you?"

"Who knows." Juri tilted her head. "When I got back to the hotel, I went by the front so someone might have seen me. I didn't think something like this would happen."

"I understand. That's okay."

I looked over the notepad in my hand. That meant the people who had likely seen Juri were the restaurant waitress, the convenience store employee, and the Polar Hotel staff. But if I took her for her word, then during that time she hadn't had any conversations that would leave an impression on anyone.

"The problem is when there's a public criminal investigation. If your profile shot went around the metropolitan area, one of those people you just brought up might remember you."

"Impossible."

"I think so too, but it's when that impossibility happens to occur that a premeditated crime fails. We can't be relaxed."

"Then what should we do?"

"All we can do is put a nail in it before your photo goes public. Although it's unsophisticated, it's likely we'll be telling them that line."

"That line?"

"There's a line that you often hear in kidnapping dramas, isn't there? *If you tell the police, your kid's as good as dead.* It's so clichéd that it's embarrassing."

"Ah. But isn't that something you need to say anyway?"

"Why?"

"Well…"

I put down the notepad and poured the remaining wine into my glass. I crossed my legs up on the sofa. "No matter what I say, your father will go to the police. He's that kind of person. So there's no point in telling him, *Don't go to the police.* It's a frill. It's something I'd love to have left out if I could."

Juri was silent. She seemed to know that Katsutoshi Katsuragi wasn't the type to be frightened by a kidnapper's threats.

"Then again, even if I don't say that stuff, I don't think the police would go public with it. It's just in case. More than that, we need to think about what happens afterwards. You'd be safely protected, but you can't recklessly expose yourself to the paparazzi. For the reason I just gave. We don't know who might have seen you between yesterday and today."

At that she turned her wide eyes to me. "You're already thinking about the aftermath?"

"Naturally. Without an idea of the final shape of things, we couldn't ever hatch a plan to get us there."

"And that final shape is you and I winning?"

"Needless to say. I always try to picture victory, or rather, I'm the kind of guy who can't picture things any other way." I tilted my glass and savored the bitterness of the red wine.

"If it goes well, I plan on going abroad. So I don't intend to subject myself to the media or be interviewed."

"Fine, though completely shutting out reporters will be hard.

But they'll probably agree to a request not to show your face."

"Yeah, I'll do that," she consented docilely, which was unlike her.

"Then let's say that we've resolved the matter of who witnessed you after you ran away from home." I took the notepad and pen in my hands again. "Tell me about what happened before you ran away from home. It's important."

"Before I ran away?"

"Yesterday night, I only saw you as you left. I want you to tell me where you were until then and what you did. If you can, tell me about your behavior in detail throughout the day."

"I suppose that's important, too?"

"Would I ask if it wasn't?" I tapped the pen's point against the pad twice. "You got this? With a kidnapping, the police will first try to figure out when and how you were abducted. That's because they have a good chance of putting together a profile of the perp from those conditions. Long story short, if no one could have kidnapped you, they might start suspecting it's a charade."

Juri had a long face. But it seemed she'd understood what I said. "I didn't really meet with anyone yesterday," she offered.

"Please don't be vague like that. That won't be useful at all."

She glared at me indignantly. "I can't help it."

"Then, let me ask you this way. Who did you last see?"

"That would be…" Juri tilted her head to think, and answered without righting it. "Chiharu…I guess."

"Who is that?"

"Papa's second wife's kid."

"Ah, your half-sister. So her name's Chiharu. How do you write it?"

"'Thousand' and 'spring' as in the season." She snorted. "What an uncool name."

"I don't think it's so bad. So, when did you see her? In the house, right?"

"After dinner. Around eight. I was at the bathroom sink, and Chiharu came in. We didn't exchange any words, though, I don't think."

"And then?"

"I went to my room and watched TV. Like always. I'm always by myself like that 'til morning."

"You really didn't see anyone? It's really important so try to remember."

Juri shook her head, like she couldn't bother to. "After dinner, everyone holes up in their own room, so normally I don't see anyone. Chiharu always seems to be sleeping over somewhere, but I don't think her parents know. She just needs to be back in her room by breakfast."

Just four family members in that huge mansion—perhaps it made sense. "So you ate with your mom and Chiharu, just the three of you?"

Katsutoshi Katsuragi would have been in the middle of a business dinner with Kozuka at that time. Tasting expensive dishes, he must have ordered that the incompetent Shunsuke Sakuma be dropped from the project.

"I was alone during dinner."

"Alone? Why?"

"It seemed like the two of them had gone out. That kind of thing happens a lot. I find it more comfortable, though."

"So did you prepare dinner by yourself?"

I'd have been a little surprised, but she quickly shook her head. "Of course not. Ms. Saki makes it for us. Oh, that's right. Ms. Saki was there during dinner."

"Ms. Saki? That's a name that hasn't come up yet."

"She's our helper. She commutes all the way from Osaki."

So they had a house servant. That was only natural, come to

think of it.

"When are her working hours?"

"I don't know exactly, but I think she usually comes around the afternoon. She does the cleaning and laundry, and buys the groceries, and also makes dinner. She goes home at different times depending on the day, but usually before dinner. Yesterday, though, I think she was cleaning up the kitchen while I was eating."

"So after you finished eating, she went home."

"I assume she did."

"During dinner, did you talk?"

"Of course we did. We couldn't just be together and not speak, could we?"

"What did you talk about? Nothing hinting at running away from home, I hope?"

"Why would I? I didn't mean to at that point."

"I see." I circled Chiharu's name, which I had written on the notepad. "You told me yesterday about why you were done with the Katsuragis, but I thought there had to be some reason for your impulsive escapade. It seems your talking to Chiharu after dinner was it. Didn't something happen then?"

For a moment, Juri's face became like a mask. She folded her arms, then pouted. "She complained that I used the cream."

"The cream?"

"The cosmetic cream. I just borrowed a little from the one in the washroom."

"A-ha." I nodded. "And then you had an argument."

"We didn't. We don't quarrel. Times like that, I just apologize, it's on me. I'm used to it because it happens all the time. But yesterday she was a little persistent. She kept on complaining no matter what."

"So you got pissed off and ran away from home?"

"After I got to my room, I just got more and more frustrated. I suppose you could say I felt miserable. Anyway, I didn't want to be in that house for a second longer."

Just like a grade school kid, I thought, but I held my tongue.

Looking at my notes, I tried to organize the info. I'd have to think of a story that didn't contradict the material she'd given me.

"You said Chiharu sometimes stays over somewhere. What about you? You ran away from home yesterday, but have you ever slipped away to go out like her?"

"It's not like I haven't ever. But not as frequently as Chiharu. I have the right to enjoy my best years, too."

"Your best years, huh." If a thirty-something man threw that out, it'd probably reek of old age, but why did it sound so fresh coming out of a young woman's mouth? "And for that, you climb over the wall like you did yesterday?"

"I usually leave through the back door. But last night I didn't want to be on the security camera no matter what, so I went for the wall. Depending on the camera angle, it'd show me if I went out the back door."

"Going out is no piece of cake, huh? Did you ever stay out overnight?"

"I might have...a few times." Looking like she was recalling those instances, she shrugged her shoulders.

"I forgot a crucial bit. Do you have a boyfriend?"

"Right now I'm single. It's like whenever people find out I'm a daughter of the Katsuragis, they keep their distance."

"Students these days haven't got any guts. They should have a go at hitching themselves to a princess. So the people you go out with are girlfriends?"

"Well, yeah. College friends and stuff."

"When you go out, you get in touch with them first, I presume?"

"Yeah. But sometimes I just go out on a whim. If I try the places where I'm a regular, I usually recognize a face or two."

For a little young lady of twenty to claim "regular" status was saucy. But now I could attach an explanation to her sneaking out at night.

"By the way," I said, turning my eyes to her bag again, "do you have your cellphone with you?"

"I left it. Because it's a bother."

"A bother?"

"Because if they found out I was missing, they'd call me. If it kept going off, it'd be annoying. If I'd have to turn it off anyway, there'd be no point in having it. If I wanted to make a call, I could just use a public phone anyway."

"I like your logical thinking," I approved, nodding a few times. It wasn't flattery. "But because of that, there's one problem. If you left without your cellphone, the police would probably have doubts."

"Wouldn't they simply think I forgot it?"

"Would young women nowadays ever forget their phone when they go out? Maybe even their wallets, but their phones? The detectives would find it odd. Our question is how to clear that."

"Everyone forgets their phone once in a while, when they're in a hurry."

"Then why were you in a hurry? You didn't even have a promise to meet someone."

"Because I wouldn't make the last train?"

I snorted. "You, who took a cab from near your house? But the idea that you 'wouldn't make it' isn't bad." I tapped the notepad twice with my pen. "You said you have several places you frequent. Are there any that close at midnight among those?"

Juri gave this some thought, biting lightly on the nail of her thumb, before her lips parted. "Shibuya's 'Doubt' might."

"Okay, then let's go with that. Chiharu bitching about the cosmetic cream pissed you off. You decided to fix your mood by going to Doubt. But if you didn't hurry, it'd close. You were in a rush and forgot your phone. Anything seem unnatural so far?"

"Nope," she answered, without giving it any deep consideration.

I wasn't relying on her judgment to begin with. "Next is when and where the culprit kidnapped you."

This was the big problem. If we bumbled here, the plan would be ruined.

I ran a simulation in my mind. I was the perp trying to abduct a Katsuragi girl. Where would I ambush her and get away without being seen?

"It seems like only one place would offer a chance. After you snuck out of the mansion, you went out to the road and hailed a taxi. If someone were kidnapping you, it'd happen before you got out to the road. The street was dark, and there weren't any passersby at that hour. They could only abduct you then."

"By abduct, you mean I'd have been taken by force?"

"In an instant, before you even had the time to scream." At that point I closed my eyes and pictured the scene. The high-end residential area of Denenchofu. Juri walking on her own. The kidnapper approaching her from behind in a car. Slowly. When they passed her, they would stop. Opening the back door, a man would quickly disembark.

"There would have to be at least two," I said with my eyes still shut. "The driver, and another guy on standby in the backseat. Getting out of the car, the latter would put a handkerchief over your mouth as you stood frozen in surprise. That handkerchief would have the standard chloroform on it—" I shook my head. "Chloroform is so clichéd. Ether, then. It's used for inhaled anesthesia. The kidnapper has medical knowledge and knows how to handle it."

"Does it matter which? It's stuff the police can't look into anyway."

I opened my eyes and showed her a frown. "It has to do with my constructing an image. I have to figure out the details of the crime and work out the culprits' characters as well."

"Do you really need to go that far?" Juri mocked me.

"Staged kidnappings fall apart because the perps haven't imagined how it would go if it weren't staged. They end up acting in weird ways that seem all but staged and give themselves away. Why do you think I was prying into what you were up to before you ran away?"

I wasn't sure if Juri took my point, but she mutely raised and lowered her shoulders.

I decided to go on. "The kidnappers who knocked you out with the ether make a quick getaway in the car. Their destination is a hideout they secured in advance. There they have enough food and an assortment of daily necessities. Naturally, they have a phone line, plus a computer. They also have a TV set. They can stay holed up for days with you in captivity."

"And the location of the hideout?"

"That's pretty important. We can't choose carelessly. We have to think about where their hideout would be alongside coming up with the perps' personalities."

"If it's all the same, make them cool."

"Unless it's necessary, we won't. For instance, one of their traits would be that they're incredibly cautious and tenacious, but at the same time, when they do act, they're swift and bold."

"Huh, is that right."

"Think about it. Given the abduction method, the perps somehow learned that the Katsuragi girls occasionally slipped out of the house, and kept lookout on the estate waiting for a chance. They wouldn't do that if they weren't cautious and tenacious. At the same time, when the chance did arise, they didn't hesitate. That means they also have the power to act."

"I see." Juri gave a slight nod and looked at me with upturned eyes. "Can I ask one thing?"

"What is it?"

"Am I all tied up at the hideout?"

"I'm trying to decide if you would be or if you're just being held there. What about it?"

"Um…" She licked her lips and said, "Do I get raped there?"

5

To Mr. Katsutoshi Katsuragi,

We have your dear daughter. If you would like her returned safely to you, then abide by our demands. First, prepare   hundred million yen in cash.

This goes without saying, but do not contact third parties or the police. If you do not uphold this, the deal is off.

Note that we have not done your daughter physical harm, but depending on her attitude, there are limits to our chivalry. We believe a quick decision would be best for both of us.

I swiveled my chair a half-turn toward Juri. "So, how much should we make the ransom?"

After having peered at the computer screen, she had sat back down on the bed. "I take it you're going to make it over one hundred million yen?"

I smiled. "Why not? Who do you think got kidnapped? The daughter of world-renowned Nissei Automobile's executive vice president. We can't demand less than a hundred million, that'd be chump change."

"I wonder if they would pay that much. For a child by a mistress."

"The kidnappers wouldn't know that."

I swiveled back my chair and rested my hands on the keyboard. In the empty blank of [hundred million yen] I typed the number [3].

"Three hundred million yen? Why?" Juri asked.

"No particular basis. If I must say, to throw them off." I reached for my can of beer. "It might have the effect of making them wonder if the kidnappers are a trio. These days, three hundred million yen perhaps isn't a whole lot, but if we made it ten or twenty, even your father wouldn't be able to gather that much right away."

"So…three hundred million yen. If we split it, that's one-point-five hundred million yen each."

"I'm okay with just a tenth. Thirty million yen. The one who needs money is you."

"You don't need money?"

"I do. But the goal of this game isn't just that."

I operated the mouse. A colorful 3D image appeared on the screen. On the top was a title. It said "AUTOMOBILE PARK."

"What is that?"

"The fruits of months of labor. If some blockhead nutcase hadn't interfered, this dream of a world would have become reality."

I clicked with the mouse. A digital gate opened, revealing a world of automobiles. If you continued to the right, you could see the invention's early days. From cars that used steam engines, to classics, an assortment of gems that would make an aficionado drool.

"It's like a museum."

"It's not just a museum. Those places always have warnings, don't they. *Patrons, please do not touch the exhibits.* But at this automobile park, there are no tasteless warning signs. On the contrary, the patrons can test-drive all the cars. From ones that require you to hand-crank the engines to Toyota 2000 GTs and F1s, you can ride anything. Even without a license."

"How?"

"Each area has several simulators. With them, you can virtually experience riding any car you wish. In a nutshell, it's like an arcade driving game. Even the scenery changes by make and model. Say, for the Toyota 2000 GT, it's set up so you feel like you're driving around in the good old Showa era."

"Huh, sounds fun." Juri seemed genuinely impressed. If only her father had been as simple.

"Coming into contact with the history of automobiles, the patrons gradually approach our own times. Past that area, you enter a speculative future auto world, but there's a special corner right before it. Frankly, that's the centerpiece. Nissei Automobile's new car is concealed in this corner. The simulator installed here lets you experience riding in the new model before anyone else. The simulator here's amazing. Unlike the toys in the other areas, it's the real deal brought in from Nissei's R&D department. Patrons will be able to verify the new car's performance as if they were actually driving it. Its image video and music would play at the same time, even as technical advisers rapid-fire its advantages. By the time you've left this special corner, pamphlet in hand, you're wondering how you might take out that loan."

I'd been speaking breathlessly, but noticing how Juri was staring at my face, I stopped. Then I sighed and switched the screen back to the ransom letter.

"I'll say this again, but if it weren't for that cranky old man of yours, everything I just talked about would be reality. Nissei Automobile's new car would have been a marketing success, and Cyberplan's stock would've risen. It would have made everyone happy."

"So basically you're causing an abduction ruckus out of spite because your plan was chopped?"

"If you're interpreting it as revenge, that's unfortunate. I told you from the start, didn't I? This is a game. I've challenged your geek of a father to a match. It's to find out once and for all who is the master."

"But Papa doesn't know it's a game. Isn't that unfair?"

"Uh-uh. Katsutoshi Katsuragi wouldn't leave this up to the police. He's bound to scheme and strategize in his own way. Of course he won't know that I'm his opponent, but make no mistake, he'll play. The real battle begins then."

I reread the ransom letter on the screen.

I'd considered various phrasings for the last bit that went [we have not done your daughter physical harm], set off by Juri's question about whether she'd be raped by the perps.

Having trapped an attractive girl of her age in a room, the kidnappers would no doubt be visited by uncouth desires. According to my setup, the kidnappers were two men. Perhaps it made better sense for one or both of them to rape the hostage if only to crush her will to flee.

But I couldn't get myself to go along with a scenario where the kidnappers violated Juri. Of course, actually doing so wasn't an option. I didn't have any interest in that. But in that case, she would have to lie. Once it was over—assuming our crime was successful, of course—the police would ask her about every little thing. Did the kidnappers lay a hand on you? In short, they would be sure to inquire if they'd had their way with her. What would be the best reply for her? How did hostages who were actually treated in such a way respond? This was the hard part. If she didn't give a straight answer, wore a bitter expression, and teared up, the detectives might infer what had happened. But the issue was whether Juri could act. I decided I couldn't expect that. It wouldn't do to underestimate the investigators' insight.

The kidnappers did not commit rape—that was the conclusion I reached. Then why had they thought better of it? Abstaining of their own accord wasn't exactly persuasive. The idea I came up with was almost contrived.

The kidnappers were a team of two, and one was a woman. They were lovers or even married. When they kidnapped Juri, the woman was driving. With this setup, even if the woman wasn't watching, the man would be highly unlikely to go after Juri.

The words "we have not done your daughter physical harm" were meant to imply rape, but also the perps' unwillingness to do such a thing. Finding out from Juri's mouth afterwards that one of the kidnappers was a woman, the detectives would slap their knees.

"Now, the next question is how to send the ransom letter." I folded my arms and leaned back in my chair. "Do you know your father's email?"

"I don't," Juri readily admitted with a shake of her head.

"What about his cellphone number?"

She showed me her outspread palms in reply.

"You don't know anything, huh?"

"Well, go to Shibuya and ask girls around my age. Ask if they remember their dad's email or cellphone number. If you ask ten girls and even one of them answers yes, then I'll kiss your feet."

"I don't particularly want you to kiss my feet."

Maybe that's true, though, I thought. As it was, recording people's numbers and such in our phones was making us remember the info less and less. That was true even for me. What's more, she probably rarely called her father.

It wasn't like I didn't have the means to look up Katsutoshi Katsuragi's email and phone number. Asking someone at the company was all it took. However, I'd have to give my name.

"You can't just call?" Juri asked. "In kidnapping dramas and stuff, don't the kidnappers usually call?"

"If we do that, then we take on a huge risk. Being traced is out of the question, but the kidnapper's voice, voice print, speech pattern, the background noise, all of that is of value to police and gives them an upper hand. If we make a blunder like that from the start, a perfect crime is a dream of a dream."

"But it's the first call. I don't think the police are on this yet. Our home phone doesn't even have voicemail."

"Twenty hours have passed since you left home. We have to assume that they've contacted the police. Police take all possibilities into account. If this were a normal home, they might leave it alone, but the person who disappeared is Katsutoshi Katsuragi's daughter. They must be considering the abduction scenario, and several investigators are probably waiting for the perp to call."

"I wonder if they would do all that," Juri said, tilting her head.

"Maybe they haven't, but maybe they have. I'm no optimist, so I don't make bets on fifty-fifty chances." I looked at the computer screen. I had thought I could send the ransom letter by email, but that seemed to be out. "You have a fax, I'm sure?"

"We do. In Papa's study. Are you faxing it?"

"That seems least likely to give our opponents a clue. Okay, next is how we get their reply. Any ideas?"

I asked Juri without expecting her to come up with a decent plan, but she started thinking with a serious look on her face.

"It seems like you were going to send the ransom letter by email at first, but what address were you planning on using? You weren't thinking of using the one you normally use."

"Of course not. No fool would be honest enough to provide his name and address to send a ransom letter. I can make the receiver's software show a fake address, but just in case, I was going to prepare a new address."

"An address that won't give you away?"

"Right. There are two options I'm considering. One is a free email service." On Hotmail, for instance, I could acquire an account without a clear identity or address. Even the police had no chance of figuring out who I was from such an account.

"And the other option?"

I pointed at Juri's chest. "Using your address."

"Mine?"

"You use email too, don't you?"

"I remember the address, but I forgot the password."

"In that case, let's make a new one. You said you have a credit card, right? As long as you do, you can sign up right away."

"Huh." Juri looked pensive for some reason. "One correction."

"What's that?"

"I was lying about having a card. I just have some pocket money, that's all."

"I suspected as much. Why did you lie?"

"I didn't want to show you a chink in my armor. If I told you I didn't have money, I'd be showing a weakness."

I glared at her face as Juri confessed this shamelessly, but she was unperturbed. "If that's the case, then we only have one option. I guess we'll use a free email service."

"You're getting an account at one of those?"

"What about it?"

"Well, you can provide that address on the ransom letter and tell them to email their reply when you fax them."

"That's one way." I felt like cutting the girl some slack. She was pretty sharp.

"But we can't do that?"

"It's not bad, but it's not fun. I don't feel like communicating with my opponent by email. Even if we do get an account, we'd use it just once. We'd obtain another one to send a new email. In short, if the opponent tried to email us, we wouldn't see it."

"How cautious of you."

"Naturally. What do you think we're up to here?"

I took the TV remote in my hand and turned it on. The wide screen displayed a basketball match. I started changing the channel. A Nissei Automobile commercial played during an interlude in a sports program. It was for a sports car called the CPT. A popular female celebrity coolly drove through grasslands. Not a particularly well-made ad, it probably hadn't been checked in advance by Katsutoshi Katsuragi.

I faced the computer and connected to the internet. I used a search engine and tried looking up a website for the CPT. Sure enough, there were fans who had barged ahead and made a page. I went to one of them and peeked at its contents. The title of it was "CPT Owners Club." First, a red CPT appeared at the top of the screen. It was an amateurish photo, most likely of the ride of the page's creator. "A place where people who love the CPT can exchange info and relax. Please feel free to look around," it said. The pages listed were "Latest Updates," "Maintenance," "My CPT Photos," and "Bulletin Board." What a great age, where anyone could transmit information. I clicked on "Bulletin Board." Without delay, the posts appeared as follows:

Looking forward to it (hummingbunny)
Hello everyone. I told you all before, but a CPT will finally be coming to my house. I'm already imagining the feeling of hurtling down the highway and I haven't been able to sleep for days. After I take my first ride, I'll report back immediately. Hopefully I won't get into an accident. (lol)

Weird noise (sparkleprincess)
I've been driving a CPT for two years now. Lately, I've been worried about the thermometer being high. I'm afraid of it overheating. Is anyone else having the same experience?

RE: Weird noise (streetracersamurai)
sparkleprincess, my beloved car has been showing similar symptoms. It seems that the CPT's physique (?) puts

pressure on the radiator. But it's never overheated. If you're worried, you could try getting it inspected (sucky advice, I know).

The people, who had been given a toy called the internet, were dribbling their infantile, sickly sweet sentences as usual. But exactly the same types might be spewing savage and nefarious words elsewhere. They were best left alone.

I saved the URL and, for the time being, disconnected.

I pulled the ransom letter from earlier up on the desktop. After looking at it for a while, I continued it as follows:

> If you intend to comply with the transaction, access the URL below and use Juri's name on the bulletin board to state your intent. Upon confirmation, you will receive a response.
>
> Site name: CPT Owners Club
> URL: http://www...

"How's that?" I turned around and looked at Juri.

After reading it over several times, she nodded her head up and down. "I see. It won't make anyone suspicious, and you'll be able to confirm their intent."

"Kidnappers in the past often used newspapers. They'd demand a classified in one of the major dailies, with copy like 'So-and-so: Problem solved, come home asap.' But with that, you have to wait until the next day. By using an internet bulletin, we can obtain confirmation immediately, and more than anything, it's cheaper for the victim. It's become a convenient world."

I turned on the printer and tried printing.

"Wait a second," Juri said, placing her hand on my shoulder.

"What is it?"

"I have just one request for the ransom letter."

"A complaint, miss?"

"I'm not satisfied with the 'your dear daughter' part. Write my name properly. Say 'Juri.'"

I read the wording over again. Then I shook my head. "We can't. If it's 'Juri' then it feels slack. Why not 'your dear daughter'?"

"I'm not their dear daughter," she insisted, facing down.

"I'll say this again, but the kidnappers don't know about your upbringing. They think of you as the Katsuragis' precious girl. I don't think it'd be unnatural for them to put it that way. In fact, calling you 'Juri' would be odd."

"Anyway, I don't want it like that."

I sighed. "Then how about 'your daughter'? That'd be fine, yes?"

But she wouldn't nod. "I'm Juri. Juri Katsuragi. I'm not really their daughter."

"What a pain…" The girl was giving me a headache. "Fine. Then it'll be 'Juri Katsuragi.' I won't add 'Miss.' No honorifics. Agreed? That's the most I'll compromise."

Juri nodded slowly. "Agreed."

I shrugged my shoulders, then tapped on the keyboard and modified the text. Damn if I understood how girls her age felt.

I read through the ransom letter again, and verifying that there were no typos, I printed it out. After checking the ink quality, I handed it to Juri.

"You're sending this with an actual fax machine? Not your computer's fax modem?"

"Just in case. I don't want them specifying my computer from the document format. Also, in my experience, faxing a document of this length takes no time at all. If something happens, the line can be killed quick, too."

With a pair of scissors, I carefully cut off the margins in order not to eat up extra transmission time. Then I sliced the sheet into eight pieces at random.

"What are you doing?"

"Well, just watch."

Pulling out cellophane tape, I reassembled the pieces in a haphazard order with some facing the wrong way. I set the patchwork in the fax next to the computer.

"You're sending it from here?" Juri asked in a surprised voice. "Won't they trace it?"

"I made it into this patchwork so they won't. Even if police are waiting at the Katsuragi household, they won't know what it is at first, right? Once they put together the jigsaw puzzle and realize it's a ransom letter, the phone will have hung up." I looked right at Juri. "My contract for this phone withholds the caller ID, so as long as I don't press 186 beforehand, the number doesn't show up on the other side. Now then, let's have you dial. You're going to send this fax yourself."

"Why are you having me send it?"

"I want you to be aware you're complicit in this crime. You said you'd go along with my plan, but once you actually have to commit to it yourself, you might balk. I can't have you saying you changed your mind after I've sent the ransom letter."

There, I pointed at the fax.

Juri bit her lower lip. She glared at me. I just sat on my chair and looked back at her. My own way of doing things was to secure an out even if I was attempting something risky.

Juri exhaled. "I have something that I want to do before sending the fax."

"Are you going to take a shower and cool your head?"

"I want to go to my house."

"A-ha." I made a disappointed face. "Are you missing home after getting this far? In that case, it can't be helped." I took the ransom letter out from where it was set in the fax and made to tear it apart and throw it away.

"Wait, it's not that. It's not that I want to go home. I just want to see it from outside."

"Same difference, you're balking. If you're like that, we can't win this game."

"I told you it's not like that. You just don't get it." Losing her patience, Juri shook both her hands. "I don't intend to run away from this game. I want revenge on that family, too. What I want to check is whether Papa is in the house. Because if you send that fax when he isn't, then it's meaningless. Like I told you, the fax machine is in his study, and no one can touch it without permission."

"Hunh." I returned the ransom letter back to the fax's top. "But it's not like your dad wouldn't ever come home. He would sooner or later and notice the fax."

"But I don't like not knowing when that'll be. Until I know Papa's read the ransom letter, I won't be able to calm down and sleep."

I put my index finger in my ear and scratched inside. I understood how she felt. "You wouldn't know whether he's home just by looking from outside, though."

"I'll check the garage. If he's home, his car will be there."

"I see." I could only agree. "Is the fax combined with the phone? Or is it—"

"Its own line. One digit different from the phone."

"When a fax is sent, is there a ring?"

Juri shook her head. "There shouldn't be."

"Then even if Mr. Katsuragi is home, he might not read the ransom letter until tomorrow morning. He'd be asleep at this hour."

"I want to check that, too. It's been more than twenty-four hours since I left home, right? I want to see with my own eyes if they're still going on with their daily lives like nothing happened."

"If the house's lights are all completely on, then everyone's worried, you feel moved, and you bail?" I asked in my best sarcastic voice.

"I don't think I'd ever, so I want to go see. Plus, it can't be bad for the plan, either, to see how the house is before dispatching the ransom letter."

"What's so good about it?"

"We'd be able to check if the police are on standby."

I laughed. "You think they parked some patrol cars in front of the house?"

"If there are detectives, wouldn't the house have lights on at least?"

"That's…" I couldn't say there wasn't some truth to it. "But it's dangerous. The police would definitely notice a suspicious car parking nearby. And your house has security cameras, too. If we get caught by those, then it's all for nothing."

"We can just go past the front. That wouldn't be suspicious."

I growled and folded my arms. I looked her in the face again. "What if I said no?"

"Then"—she shrugged her shoulders—"it can't be helped. Do things your way. But I won't send the fax."

"Point taken."

I stood up and went to the window. I opened the curtain a little and gazed down at the nighttime city.

Push or relent? If Juri was having second thoughts, I should probably abort this game. But to judge from her expression reflected in the glass, she didn't seem scared. The girl had a devil-may-care attitude from the start, and it had been decisive in my coming up with this game.

I turned back to her. "We need a disguise."

"A disguise?"

"We won't risk the one-in-a-million chance of them noticing you in the car."

She seemed to take my meaning and nodded with a smile.

About forty minutes later, Juri and I were in a taxi. I didn't use my own car because I was afraid of leaving any evidence on the cameras.

En route, we conversed just to the extent that it wouldn't seem unnatural. Our topics were soccer, TV dramas. We couldn't come across to the driver as a suspicious couple. Fortunately, he didn't seem to take any interest in us. Juri wore a jean jacket over a sweatshirt. They were both very puffy, but more than enough young people dressed weirder. I was wearing a leather jacket. To the driver, we were probably a dumb couple idly amusing ourselves in the middle of the night.

The cab entered the Denenchofu residential area. Juri gave detailed directions in my stead. As the Katsuragi residence approached, sweat sprung on my palms.

Finally, we saw the mansion ahead of us, on the right. But it wasn't like we could have the car slow down.

"Just keep going straight like this, please," Juri told the driver. She put the hood of the sweatshirt over her head. She also pulled together the front of her jean jacket and drew her chin in to bury her face.

Without losing speed, the car went by the Katsuragi estate on the gate side. In that short amount of time, we focused our eyes to observe the state of the house.

After we'd passed it, Juri and I faced each other. She gave a slight nod, so I did too. It seemed that all the lights in the mansion were off.

At a random spot, we got out of the taxi, walked a little, and then flagged another. On the way back, we were both silent.

Having returned to my condo, we faced each other again by the fax machine.

"Either way, the lights in your house were all off," I said. "What about the car?"

"It looked like Papa's was there. If I didn't see wrong, that is."

"In other words, Katsutoshi Katsuragi is home. He's asleep in that house, then. While we're at it, there didn't seem to be any police for now." I looked at the fax. "If we're sending the ransom letter, this is the best time to do it."

"Can't it wait 'til morning?"

"With a new day, the situation will change. And you'll feel anxious again. Now's the time to send it. If we're wasting this opportunity, the game is off."

Juri was looking at the ransom letter, thinking. I glanced at the clock on the wall. I intended to give her ten minutes. Giving her more time to decide was useless.

Five minutes into the continued silence, she raised her face. "Got it. I'm sending it."

"You can't take it back."

"You better not get cold feet, yourself."

"Want another toast? A pledge over a drink."

Juri shook her head and stepped in front of the fax machine. Checking that the letter was set and the status was on-hook, she reached her fingertips toward the number buttons.

6

After spending several hours not knowing whether I was asleep or awake, I got up from the sofa. Like usual, I did my calisthenics, pushups, and sit-ups. As I was sprawled on the floor, trying to catch my breath, Juri's face appeared above me. "Good morning."

"You're up early. Or could you not sleep?"

"I'm hungry."

"Just wait. I'll make something now." I got up and went to the kitchen.

The morning menu I decided on was toast, boiled eggs, and vegetable juice. Putting on coffee was a bother.

Nibbling on toast, I started up the computer and checked my email. There were just two. Both of them were trivial messages. Because the automobile park had been scrapped, they were trying to get rid of me as though I were a has-been. I couldn't let that happen. I would make a comeback no matter what.

Sensing eyes on me, I turned around to Juri staring at the computer screen. I asked her what she wanted.

"I wonder if Papa saw it," she said haltingly.

"Do you want to check?"

"Yeah."

I double-clicked the browser icon at the top of the computer. I accessed the CPT Owners Club URL and checked out the bulletin board.

Since the time I'd gone there the night before, there were two new entries. Neither of them seemed like a message from Katsutoshi Katsuragi.

"There's still no reply," I said, closing the browser window.

"Maybe he hasn't seen it?"

"I doubt that. If he keeps a fax machine in his study at home, he's making the assumption that someone will contact him in an emergency. After he wakes up, he'd normally go check if something's come in first thing. He must be staring at the ransom letter right now thinking of what to do." I looked at the clock. It had just passed eight o'clock.

I left the computer and washed down the rest of the toast and boiled egg with vegetable juice.

"Let me predict what your father will do from here on. First, he'll contact the police. He's a man with quite some status, so he probably knows one or two people with a close police connection. I'd say an expert kidnapping investigator from the Tokyo Metropolitan Police Department would arrive at their house within an hour. In that time, your father will call his office to tell them that he won't be coming in today due to personal business. Furthermore, he'll warn them not to call him at his home unless it's really urgent. He'll call the help and tell her she doesn't have to come in today, and order his wife and other daughter not to leave the premises. Well, something like that."

"What about contacting the bank?"

"Are you talking about the ransom? Not yet. That's after he's talked to the police. And this is Katsutoshi Katsuragi. He already knows exactly how to prepare a sum like three hundred million yen. He's probably at no loss for a helpful face at the bank."

I went to the bathroom, took a quick shower, and while shaving, thought of what to do going forward. For now, Katsutoshi Katsuragi would probably post on the web page. There was no mistaking his reply would pertain to the deal, but I didn't think it would end there. He'd give conditions. *I want to confirm my daughter is safe*, and stuff like that. How would I respond to that?

When I got back to the room after brushing my teeth, Juri was sitting on the sofa watching TV. It seemed to be a news program.

"Are you going to work?" she asked.

"Believe it or not, I have a day job."

"What should I do in the meantime?"

"I want to say do what you like, but if you do, I'd be in trouble. First, don't leave this room. That's the most important thing. If someone calls over the intercom, ignore it. Don't make or answer any phone calls. Keep those promises, and you can do whatever you want here."

"I'll get hungry."

"There's pilaf in the freezer and there's prepackaged and canned food in the cupboards. Sorry, but make do with that for today. You can drink the wine and beer, but don't go overboard. It'd be a bother if you got drunk and did something weird."

"I can't go to the convenience store either?"

"Just think of what we're trying to do. It's not plain hide-and-seek." I put up my index finger. "Correction. It's not what we're trying to do anymore. It's what we're doing. The game's already begun. We've crossed the line."

Juri gave back a sharp look as though to say, *I know that*. We were good as long as she could make such a face.

I left the condo and got on the subway like usual. I looked at my reflection in the glass and was satisfied. No matter how you looked at it, it was the face of a man going to work. I didn't see someone perpetrating a kidnapping and blackmailing a family. In what kind of world did a kidnapper head to work in an Armani suit?

In my humble opinion, crime wasn't such a big deal. Mercenary crimes, in particular, were no different from work. Instead of trying to come up with ways to evade a net of legalities, you took precautions not to get caught in the police's radar. Blackmail was the same as a deal. In fact, compared to negotiations with stubborn clients, it was almost simple fun.

I told Juri we'd crossed a line, but I didn't really think that was the case. If it started to look too risky, I could just hurry and retreat. Keeping Juri from talking wasn't hard. She, herself, would want to hide her involvement in a staged kidnapping. I wasn't scared even about getting caught. I'd just say that she'd talked me into going along with her prank. She'd assert that I was the one who suggested it, but she'd have no proof. And then this was the biggest thing: the victim, Katsutoshi Katsuragi, would probably be afraid of the public finding out the truth.

Of course, right now, backtracking wasn't on my mind. I'd never faced a challenge and failed. I would beat this game, too.

Boring chores awaited me at work. A movie featuring a popular girl singer and its videogame tie-up, to be sold in tandem—it was too tedious a job to be handled by a grown man. During the meeting, I was thinking of a way to retrieve the ransom money. That was far more amusing.

After getting back to my seat, I accessed the internet again on my computer. I checked the homepage, but there was no reply from Katsutoshi Katsuragi.

So he was still consulting with the police? I somewhat regretted not having set a deadline. It was quite likely that they'd stall.

"What are you looking at?" a voice came from my back.

I closed the window on my desktop even before I could guess whose voice it was. When I turned around, Sugimoto was in a half-crouch. Had he been looking at my computer screen until now?

"Did you find some fun site?" he layered it on me.

"No, I was just killing time." If this man had made out the website I'd been looking at, that spelled trouble. "I thought I'd collect some information on the idol movie."

"Ah, you mean the Yumi Kurihara vehicle where she becomes a game character?"

"Right, that."

"That's difficult."

Sugimoto had a look of pity and superiority on his face. He probably thought our positions were now completely reversed.

Anyway, I couldn't let him know what web page I'd been checking.

"Didn't you have another meeting with Nissei today?" I asked.

"Uh, we were supposed to, but I suddenly got a message that it's been canceled."

"Was it Nissei who canceled?"

"Yes. Apparently, Mr. Katsuragi wasn't going to be able to make it."

"Mr. Katsuragi?"

"I don't see why their EVP needs to be there, but as far as this project goes, we can't continue without him." Having said this, Sugimoto seemed to think he'd gone too far in my presence, and left with a *See ya*.

I tapped my desk with my fingertips. Receiving a ransom letter from kidnappers had been enough to make even Katsutoshi Katsuragi fret. Right around now, he was probably looking pale at home.

When it got to be lunch, I left the office and ate at a nearby café. Sipping coffee, I thought again about how I would get the ransom money.

Three hundred million yen had quite a bit of volume. It would probably take more than one bag to hold. Even if it didn't, carrying it would be no cakewalk.

Kidnappers got caught because they weren't smart about getting the ransom money. Conversely, for the police, that was the best time for nabbing the perp. I had to outwit the police, who'd be on guard against an array of methods.

When I got back to my workplace after finishing my coffee, the mood had shifted in some way. In particular, some of the employees were rushing about. I grabbed a junior near me and asked him if something had happened.

"Well, it's really bad. It seems Nissei Automobile's EVP is on his way."

"You mean Mr. Katsuragi? Here? Why?"

The junior shook his head. "We don't really know. Apparently there was a sudden call just now. Thanks to that, the staff on the new car campaign is panicking."

"Huh…"

I was a little confused. What was going on? What kind of person headed to work when his daughter had been kidnapped, even if it was the child of a mistress?

There seemed to be only one possibility. Katsutoshi Katsuragi still hadn't seen the ransom letter. His understanding, no doubt, was that his ill-behaved daughter was out on an unpermitted sleepover.

So the ransom letter hadn't reached him? Or it had, and he just hadn't read it? If it was the latter, it wasn't a problem, but the former would be something of a headache. I'd have to look into why it hadn't arrived.

I took the phone from my desk and called my condo. If there was some problem with the Katsuragis' fax machine, I wanted to check in with Juri. But after three rings, I remembered. I'd told her not to pick up.

I helplessly started up my computer again and accessed the internet. I visited the CPT Owners Club. I checked the bulletin board.

As soon as I did, I nearly cried out loud. It was because I found the following post:

Wish To Purchase (Julie)

Hello everyone. My name is Julie. I was invited to buy a CPT, so I tried riding one. But it was really expensive, so gathering the funds will take some time. I thought I should also inquire after the contract details.

I didn't think that a handle like Julie was a coincidence. And the text certainly seemed to be accepting the deal. In other words, this was a message from Katsutoshi Katsuragi.

As I sat there dumbfounded, someone unexpectedly patted my shoulder. It was Kozuka.

"President…"

"Sorry, while you're working, but…" He lowered his voice. "Could you come with me? I think you've heard, but Mr. Katsuragi is on his way. I want you to be present."

I grimaced. "Why me, after all that? I'm finished, no? A has-been."

Kozuka waved his hand in front of a weary face. "Now don't get nasty. Actually, Mr. Katsuragi said something strange."

"Something strange? What is it this time?"

"I don't know, but it seems he wants to see some games."

"Games?"

"Games that we handle. He's picked out about ten products and wants to hear explanations about what they're about and why they were developed. I don't really know what his aim is, but it seems to be another foothold for planning the new car campaign."

"Such a strange thing to do."

"I agree. But he says he wants to see them, so we can't not show him."

"Okay, and why am I being called too?"

"One of the games he selected is something you worked on. When we're prompted to explain it, I want you to respond."

"So that's what this is."

I sighed with resignation and stood up from my chair.

Even so, what I didn't understand was Katsutoshi Katsuragi's behavior. Responding on the bulletin board meant he'd read the ransom letter for certain. What kind of father calmly went to work when his daughter had been kidnapped? Or maybe he didn't think the ransom letter was real? He'd followed the instructions and left a reply but thought of it as nothing more than a prank? Did he mean to say that panicking about this degree of a situation was laughable?

No, that was hard to believe. It was a fact that Juri was missing, and if she still hadn't contacted them, it was only natural to think she'd been kidnapped.

Maybe it was a directive from the police. A police representative had told Katsutoshi Katsuragi, *Mr. Katsuragi, let's go about this calmly. The kidnappers wouldn't so readily lay a hand on Juri. After all, she's their valuable hostage. Things will only get worse if you panic and the press gets word of this. So, Mr. Katsuragi, please go about your day like usual. Please go to your company like usual and work like usual. If something happens, we will contact you. If your wife can stay home, that's enough. Please leave the rest to us. These kidnappers won't be making phone calls, anyway*—something of that nature.

But it worried me that he was coming to hear about games that we'd handled. What for? Could he have possibly guessed that the kidnapper worked at Cyberplan? There was no way.

As I waited in the reception room turning over various thoughts, a knock sounded and the door opened. The person who opened the door was a female receptionist, but immediately behind her was Katsutoshi Katsuragi.

Katsutoshi Katsuragi sat in an armchair with his legs crossed while he listened to Cyberplan's presentations. There was a computer with an LCD screen set up in front of him in order to describe each game and its development aims. Of course, these presentations hadn't been put together on the spot but had been made during the proposal periods. Next to the computer was a game console connected to a small TV that displayed the actual consumer-ready versions. Although a controller was also in front of Katsutoshi Katsuragi, he didn't reach for it.

Waiting for my turn, I studied his facial expressions. Although he merely glanced at each game with little interest, his questions were pointed and precise. *With what aim was this game created, why did you think it would be profitable, did you have any doubts about your sensibility*—those kinds of questions were frequent. Some of the staff were unable to answer well and became flustered. Watching the scene, it was hard to believe that Katsutoshi Katsuragi knew that his daughter had been kidnapped.

Eventually, it was my turn. The game I was to introduce was called *The Mask of Youth*.

It was a game of life, so to speak. The player was involved from the birth of the character. The computer decided, however, the parents you were born to. First, you selected which genes to receive from the mother and father and whether you were a boy or girl. After being born, you proceeded through kindergarten, elementary school, middle school, and so on, and in that time you had to choose how much to study and how much to hang out with which friends. If you assumed that you just needed to think of the future and study, you were falling into a trap. The game's biggest draw was that the character's face changed subtly depending on your life experiences.

"There's something called physiognomy," I explained to Katsutoshi Katsuragi. "It's the idea that people's faces reflect their environments and pasts. For instance, if you scan into a computer the faces of people in a particular occupation and average them, you end up with a face that's the exact image of someone working in that field. The politician's face, the banker's face, and the sex worker's face really do exist. But your destiny is not dependent on your face. Rather, your face is determined by the path you follow. One thing that makes this game enjoyable is stacking a variety of life experiences to see what face you finally get."

Katsutoshi Katsuragi opened his mouth. "The issue isn't your face, is it? To go by your own theory, the face is merely a result. I don't think people live just to come by this or that face."

"It's exactly as you say. That's why I said it's 'one thing' that makes the game enjoyable. People don't live in order to get a face—exactly. But in life, your face is important. At various crossroads, your face impacts your destiny. For instance, during job interviews. Or during matchmaking. Among girls trying to become celebrities, quite a few get plastic surgery in their teens. In this game, you'll be taking on certain crossroads with the face that your life experiences so far have shaped. Those who immersed themselves in their studies and didn't spend time with people will be emotionally warped, and it will show on their faces. They'll give a bad first impression and suffer a disadvantage in interviews and dates. *You're responsible for your face*—as the old saying goes."

"So a player who makes the wrong choice and doesn't get the face he wants just has to give up at that point?"

"In real life, it might be like that. But this is a game. In that situation, there's a secret weapon. That's the mask. At crucial moments, the hero can put on a prepared mask. It's a copy of the player's face at that point, but then you can modify it to some degree. If your face is anti-social, you can make it look somewhat more sociable. But you can use the mask only a limited number of times, and it can't be worn continuously. In the end, the player needs to strive to alter the hero's face. The ultimate goal of the game is to win happiness. In order to do so, the player has to keep exploring what kind of mask he needs."

I may have gone on for too long. I couldn't tell how Katsutoshi

Katsuragi was taking it and felt anxious. Perhaps he was in no condition to listen to anything too seriously.

"I don't know if that's a seller or not," remarked Katsutoshi Katsuragi, "but it's an interesting idea. Your experience shapes your face, which determines your destiny. In a sense, that might be the truth."

"You're too kind."

"But I wonder about being able to wear a mask during crucial moments. It might be a useful item for socially awkward youth, but there are times when suffering a setback serves you well. You could even say it's necessary."

"But this is a game."

"Even if it's a game, making them accept that they weren't up to it is important," Katsutoshi Katsuragi said, leaning back in his chair. He locked his fingers on his knees and looked up at my face. "There's one thing I'd like to ask you."

"What might that be?"

"Are you responsible for yours?"

I drew a blank for a moment. It was because I didn't understand his question. "I try to be," I said.

"So the mask you'd wear to win happiness is precisely the face you have now?"

"Maybe. It's hard to say." I faked a smile.

After scrutinizing my mask, Katsutoshi Katsuragi transferred his gaze to Kozuka. "Thank you. Next, please."

7

When I got home, Juri was cooking something in the kitchen. I tried to guess what she was making based on the smell.

"Did I have the ingredients to make cream stew?" I asked standing at the kitchen entrance.

Juri was in a shirt and sweats with a t-shirt wrapped around her hips in place of an apron. She was stirring the pot in that getup. "I scrounged through your fridge. Your vegetables were going bad, but I got to them in time."

I remembered I had bought them intending to make gratin. "You didn't meet anyone or talk on the phone?"

"Nope. I thought about how I couldn't let any of your neighbors know I was here, so I even kept the TV volume really low. I even paid attention to the sound of my footsteps. And the phone rang in the afternoon, but I didn't pick up."

That must have been my call. For now, it seemed Juri hadn't messed up.

She was paying attention to the stove's heat level. I had only used the big pot she was boiling the stew in twice.

"I didn't know you were a good cook."

"I'm not good. I was just bored. Are you hungry?"

"I already ate. I got this for you though." I lifted up a paper bag.

"What's inside?"

"A boxed meal."

She looked into the bag and then at me. "A *bento* from Yasuman. Wow. The chef there sometimes goes on TV. Then I'll have this instead."

"What about the stew?"

"Who cares now?" Juri returned to the pot and turned off the burner.

By the time I had gone into the bedroom, changed, and returned to the living room, she was starting to eat the *bento*. She admired each part, lecturing me. Working on a can of beer, I listened to her.

"By the way, I met your dad today," I said.

Her chopsticks halted. "Where?"

"He came to our company. I wonder what he's thinking when his daughter's been kidnapped. I think he's taking the police's advice, but if he wants to pretend to be calm, he could have done that at his own office."

"He doesn't care what happens to me." Juri resumed her meal.

"Regardless of what he really thinks, he knows that something's up. It seems he's seen the ransom letter. There was a reply."

"Really? On the internet?"

I turned on the computer. I connected to the internet and accessed the website. "Oh, there's another post."

In addition to the one I'd read in the afternoon was the following:

I'd like to see the quality (Julie)
I'm Julie, the newbie. I'm planning on having someone turn over their CPT to me, but I really need to see it with my own eyes, don't I? I want to check if it's damaged and I'd like to hear the sound of the engine. I feel like I shouldn't pay before I do. What do you think, everybody?

Juri had stopped eating again and was staring at the screen. I said to her profile, "So, 'what do you think,' Juri?"

"This means…"

"They need to confirm that you're safe, the deal will follow—that's the only interpretation there can be."

"What do you plan on doing?"

"Hmm, I wonder." I sat down on the sofa and stretched out my legs. I gulped down some beer. Juri was looking at me.

There were two reasons for our enemy to be saying this. One was indeed to confirm the hostage's status. The other was to obtain some clues about the culprits. What the enemy, that is to say, the police, wanted most was surely a call from the perpetrators. They would have Juri come on the phone, trace the call, and moreover try to obtain information. Right around now, the Katsuragis' phone probably had a glorified recording device attached to it, while detectives were waiting headsets in hand.

It was a mandatory scene in any novel or movie dealing with a kidnapping. The victim's family would insist on confirming the wellbeing of the hostage, and the kidnapper would exercise his wits to allow it without giving the investigators anything. You could say it was the opening skirmish between the investigators and the criminal. There was even a mystery novel where, daringly enough, the victim's state is broadcast live on TV.

It was odd, come to think of it. No reason existed for the kidnappers to grant the victim's family's request. The kidnapper only needed to keep making demands. If the deal were canceled, the victim's side had everything to lose. Hence, even in this case, I could just ignore the request. *You can confirm the hostage's safety by paying the money because she will be returned unharmed*—I could even tell them that. I thought about sending an email using those exact words. The "Julie" who wrote to the bulletin board came with an email address. Undoubtedly it was because they thought our side might email them.

"We can't call them, can we?" Juri said.

"That'd probably be fatal."

"Right."

"Do you want to call?"

She shook her head, "That's not it."

"Nowadays, I don't think even a complete idiot of a criminal would. Well, that's what I think, but actually doing something that idiotic might be fun."

"Fun…"

"Because this is a game. If it's not fun, it's not worth it. But simply making a call would be reckless."

If I were going to, I wanted it to aid us. What I wanted was to mess with the investigation. How might I do that?

"Um," Juri's lips moved slightly as I tried to puzzle it out.

"What?"

"I remembered because of the phone, but I may have done something terrible."

She sounded uncharacteristically apprehensive and timid. It gave me a bad feeling. I watched her, aware that my own gaze was sharpening.

"Yesterday, you asked me, right? After I ran away from home, whether I talked to anyone over the phone."

"Yeah. Hey, don't tell me you did." I couldn't help lifting myself from the sofa.

"I didn't talk. But I did make a call."

"What do you mean?"

"I have a friend named Yuki. Anyway, I thought I might be able to stay at her place and called her. Don't stare at me with that face. At the time, I didn't think that something like this would happen."

"All right. Keep going." My head was beginning to hurt. Young women were always like this.

"But she wasn't home. Then I remembered. Yuki was going to America starting this month. So no one came to the phone, and the answering machine message came on."

"You didn't speak into that answering machine, did you?"

Juri turned her face down with a pout at my question. I clutched my head.

"What did you say?"

"This is Juri, but I called forgetting you were in America."

"And then?"

"That's it. I hung up immediately."

I sat back down on the sofa. I frowned and stretched hard. "Why now…"

"We didn't talk. And until now I'd completely forgotten it."

"Listen, the time and date you leave a message gets recorded. When that Yuki girl gets home from America, it's a matter of time before she finds out about the kidnapping. She might look into it in detail—since it was her friend who was kidnapped. And when she hears that message on top of that? Wouldn't she wonder why you could make such a call when you were kidnapped?"

"I think it'll be okay. She's fairly easygoing, so I don't think she'd notice the time discrepancy."

I rocked my head back and forth even as she spoke. "I want to play this game perfectly. You think it's okay—do you think I can go on with nothing but vague words like that to support me?"

"Then what should we do?" Juri asked angrily.

I massaged my eyes from over my eyelids with my index finger and thumb. I was starting to feel a bit nauseous, too. "What else? We abort. This is as far as the game goes."

"But—"

"There's nothing we can do. If, by some chance, Yuki notices the time discrepancy and tells someone, what do you think will happen? The helpful someone she talks to might tell the police. The police would suspect that the kidnapping had been faked and demand an explanation from you. If that happens, that's it."

"I won't ever talk. I won't talk even if I die," Juri declared. Then she pressed her lips into a straight line as though to convey her resolve.

"Being interrogated by the police is no walk in the park. Well, it's not like I would know, but a little missy's stubbornness would be a joke to them."

Perhaps objecting to the "little missy" bit, Juri made a sour face. But I was in no state to mind her mood, either. I drained my beer dry and crumpled the empty can.

If we were aborting, then the sooner I sent her home, the better. But I couldn't just return Juri. We'd sent the ransom letter. The police had to be on the case already. My only resort would be the story that she'd talked me into playing along with her. The question was how to get her to consent to the prank narrative.

"Hey, I have a proposal," the girl offered.

"Before I listen to yours, I have a proposal myself."

"If it's a proposal to quit, then I won't listen."

I looked up at the ceiling and, like an actor in a movie, put my hands up as if surrendering.

"I was thinking of going there to erase it," Juri said, ignoring my gesture.

"Erase it? Erase what?"

"The answering machine message. If I erase that, then there's no problem, right?"

"How will you erase it? It's someone else's phone."

"She told me I could go to her room whenever I like while she's in America. She told me where she hides her key, too."

"Where does she live?"

"Yokosuka."

"Yokosuka? Why does it have to be so far away…"

"It's just a little over an hour if you go by car. We can just go there really quick and get home really fast."

"You make it sound easy. If a shady couple entered an absent resident's room, the superintendent and neighbors would definitely wonder what's going on."

"We won't be so clumsy as to be noticed. But it's better if you don't come. Because it's a women-only condo. You could just chill at Yokosuka harbor and gaze at the passing ships."

"Ridiculous." I snorted, and then remembered the time I'd visited Yokosuka.

Unexpectedly, an idea came to me.

8

Living in the metropolis, you don't really need a car. I rarely drove mine even on dates. I didn't care to abstain from drinking during the meal or for traffic jam-laced drives. What's more, my car was an MR-S. You needed to fold up the top and feel the breeze for it to shine.

In order to make a stealth round trip to Yokosuka, we couldn't take a taxi. I had Juri get in the passenger seat and left the condo's parking lot. Naturally, I left the hood up. Although the air was pretty clean outside of Tokyo, I had no intention of opening the hood this evening.

"Do you like these cars?" Juri asked right after we started driving.

"What do you mean?"

"A two-person sports car."

"Is that bad?"

"It's not that it's bad."

"It's because I have no need for three or more people to ride in it. I'm not interested in driving with men at all, and one woman at a time suits me fine."

"Where do you put your stuff?"

"There's enough room in the space behind your seat to put a Kelly bag."

"But sometimes you need to move a lot of stuff, don't you?"

"I bought this car because I wanted a mobile space. I didn't want a truck."

Juri didn't say anything to that. She may have shrugged her shoulders, but I wasn't looking at her.

"Can I listen to a CD?" she asked.

"If you like."

Just as I thought, she was narrow-minded about the music that played. "What is this? I've never heard it."

"A jazz pianist performing a Bach arrangement."

"Huh." She clearly seemed dissatisfied but didn't try to turn off the stereo.

The MR-S had no clutch. I grasped the gleaming silver lever, changed gears, and accelerated.

Just as Juri had said, about an hour after going on the Metropolitan Expressway from Hakozaki, we were getting off the Yokohama-Yokosuka Road. Past the Yokosuka Interchange, we continued onto the Honcho Yamanaka Road. A few minutes later, we were in front of Shioiri station.

"Go into that restaurant's parking lot."

Following Juri's directions, I parked the MR-S.

"Wait here. I'll go over there alone."

"Is it close?"

"It might be a short walk. But getting too close to the condo in such a flashy car is dangerous."

It was exactly as she said. I saw her off, giving her my cellphone number and telling her to call me if something happened. She crossed the wide highway and disappeared down a narrow side street.

Drinking some terrible coffee at the restaurant, I thought about how to proceed. Juri leaving a message with her friend had been a miscalculation. However, as long as we could safely erase it, there would be no problems in continuing the plan.

The biggest challenge was how to collect the cash. Three hundred million yen would be pretty bulky and heavy. In order to move it, we'd naturally need a car. But it was easy to track down a car. In the first place, going on the run with the cash was just too primitive.

If I had them change the three hundred million yen into something else with that value, I could turn it into money after getting it. For instance, I had the option of having them prepare three hundred million yen in diamonds. That way, moving it would be easy. It would be bad if someone became suspicious when I redeemed them, so I would probably need to limit each one to being worth less than one million yen. With each diamond at one million yen, that would be three hundred of them—

I shook my head. One or two, I could probably exchange, but three hundred was impossible. I could sell two at a time at different shops, but I would still have to visit a hundred fifty. Shops like that networked, so rumors of a suspicious man selling diamonds of unknown origin would probably spread quickly. I could see the detectives waiting to ambush me as I went to the fifth store.

I'd use a bank transfer then. Of course, for that I would need an account with a fictitious name, but preparing one wasn't hard. The internet is full of vendors dealing with those kinds of accounts. However, the problem was how to withdraw the money. I couldn't go to a teller, so I'd have to use an ATM. The amount I could withdraw in one day would be limited, so it would take days to extract three hundred million yen even if I made multiple accounts. The police would naturally request cooperation from banks and monitor the designated account. After using my card over a dozen times, I might get caught in the net they set. Leaving evidence on the security cameras was another worry.

It was around when I had thought up to that point. Near the register, a phone rang. A young waiter in a uniform picked up.

He looked surprised for some reason and went outside still

holding the cordless receiver. After some time, he came back and quickly disappeared behind the counter.

Eventually, a fat man who looked to be the store's manager came out with the waiter from earlier and ran outside together. When they returned, they both looked bewildered.

After consulting with each other about something, they approached the customers' tables separately. They were talking to each group of guests. In time, the young waiter came to me, too.

"Excuse me," he opened his mouth timidly.

"What is it?"

"Did you come here by car today?"

"I did, actually."

"What kind of car was it?"

"Well, it's an MR-S."

"Em-ar…" It seemed he didn't know.

"It's a navy sports car. It has a convertible hood."

The waiter's expression changed. "Um…with the Shinagawa number?"

"That's it." I had a bad feeling. I was on the edge of my seat. "Did something happen?"

"Well, it got sprayed…"

Before the waiter could finish, I ran outside.

Beholding my car, I was appalled. One of the headlights had fallen prey to red spray paint. I clucked my tongue.

"What idiot did this?"

While I stood staring at the headlight, which looked like a bloodshot eyeball, the waiter ran up to me holding something. "Um, for the time being, I brought this."

It was benzene and a towel. I didn't even feel like thanking him, but taking them, I put the benzene on the towel and tried to wipe the light. It seemed not much time had passed since it had been sprayed, and the part on the glass came off easily. However, I couldn't bring myself to scrub the painted coat. Fortunately, the damage on the body was minimal.

"Um, well." At some point the fat man who seemed to be the manager had come to stand behind me. "The restaurant is unable to take responsibility for any damages incurred in our parking lot."

"I know. I don't intend to ask for reimbursement or anything." I handed the towel and benzene to the waiter. "Thank you very much."

"Would you like to contact the police?" the waiter asked.

"No, I don't feel like making a fuss." Police presence was the last thing I wanted. "It's okay. Please go back inside." I couldn't help looking around, but there was no way the culprit would be nearby.

"Nothing like this has happened before," the fat man said by way of an excuse. I gave no reply.

I came back into the restaurant, but I didn't feel like taking my time drinking coffee, so I paid my bill and went outside. I got into the car to wait for Juri, but seeing the paint mark, I felt irritated. It was still the same new MR-S, but my affection for it was already diminished.

After about ten minutes, Juri came back. She was about to go into the restaurant, so I honked the horn once to get her attention.

When I told her about the spray paint after she got in, she looked surprised. She bothered to get back out to check on the damage.

"How terrible. I wonder if it was a motorcycle gang," she said after sitting next to me again.

"A gang these days wouldn't do something so silly. It's most likely the work of local grade school or middle school kids."

"Maybe."

"By the way, how did it go with you? Did you pull it off?"

"Perfectly." Juri made an okay sign with her fingers. "The key's hiding place hadn't changed, so getting inside was easy. And erasing the recording on the answering machine went well, too."

"And you weren't seen by anyone?"

"Do you think I'd make a mistake like that?"

"Who knows. Until just now, you'd forgotten the answering machine itself. I'd think that's a pretty big mistake."

"I remembered it and cleaned up after myself."

"After coming all the way to Yokosuka." I turned on the car engine.

After getting out of the parking lot, instead of immediately heading back, I went in the opposite direction.

"Where are you going?"

"Just stay quiet and leave it to me."

I'd come to Yokosuka in the past. Relying on those memories, I turned the steering wheel. Remembering a good portion of routes I'd taken before was something I bragged about.

I left the well-traveled highway and drove on a narrow road heading to the mountains. The houses thinned and the forest loomed closer. Finally, I saw a building illuminated by a green light diagonally in front of me. There was a parking lot sign. I slowed down.

"Wait, what are you doing?" Her tone was sharp.

"Just be quiet."

"I can't stay quiet. You never told me I'd have to go into a place like that."

I ignored Juri and parked the car on the side of the road. I put on the handbrake and cut the engine.

"Well, let's go then."

"Where?"

"Where do you think? Into that stylish building."

But Juri didn't even take off her seatbelt. She sat stiffly, facing forward, and her expression was like stone.

"You're being weird," I said, guffawing. "You've been staying with me at my place all this time. You're fine with that, but you have reservations about going into a love hotel with me?"

"But this place…"

"It's meant for a specific purpose?"

Juri didn't answer. I laughed again.

"Don't get the wrong idea. We have a lot of work to do. We need a private room."

"What work?"

"As part of our game, I mean. You thought we came all the way here just to erase a message on an answering machine?"

Relief and comprehension softened her expression. Even so, she drew her chin in distrustfully. "Then why aren't you putting the car in the parking lot?"

"Hotels like this have security cameras in the parking space that can even make out plate numbers. Considering what we're about to do, we can't leave a record of my car."

"Hmm." With an ambiguous nod, she looked at me. "You know these places well."

"I've done consulting for hotels like this in the past."

The two of us walked side by side and entered the hotel, mindful of the cameras. The room we secured had a blunt monotone interior. The first thing I did was to open the window. I'd come to the mountains, but the sea looked surprisingly close by. Occasionally, I could hear a ship whistling.

"What are you going to do here?"

"You'll understand soon. For now, could you wait over on that stylish sofa?"

But Juri didn't sit on the sofa; she took a seat on the sheeted bed. With great interest, she looked around the room, possibly because it was her first time at such a place or because it was so different from similar rooms she'd been in—I couldn't say.

I sat on the sofa and took out my notebook. With a ballpoint pen, I started writing.

"What are you writing?"

"Just wait a little."

After she bounced on the bed to get a feel for it, she used the remote on top of the table to turn on the TV. After several channels, an adult video showed up on the screen. A male actor was parting a young, naked woman's thighs and practicing some sort of mischief. Of course, the scene was censored with pixelated blurs and the crucial part wasn't visible.

Juri turned off the TV hastily. Seeing that, I chuckled.

"You're surprisingly naïve."

"I just turned it off because it was trashy. If you want to watch it, I'll turn it back on."

"No, thank you. I'm in the middle of important work."

"Huh." Juri crossed and uncrossed her legs. "Men are weird. Why does watching something like that make them so happy?"

"There are women who are fond of watching stuff like that, too."

"Not as many as men. In particular, older men are idiots. They don't even have that much pocket money themselves but spend tens of thousands of yen to date a minor. They have to be wrong in the head. Do they not get that the girl's toying with them?"

"'Toying with' sounds so predatory." My hands stopped and I lifted my face. "Are you sure about that? These older men are fools who're just being used by young girls?"

"Am I wrong?"

"Listen. Most of those guys are surviving in a harsh economy. They know more than anyone the weight of a ten-thousand-yen bill. If they're paying, it means they think it's worth it."

"But that's what—"

"If you're saying paying that much just for sex is foolish, it's not. Just a generation ago, having sex with an amateur high schooler was a dream that not even several hundred thousand yen could buy. Now, it can come true for just a few ten-thousand-yen bills. It's a

103

bargain. Not jumping on it is weird. Those older guys are thinking, 'These young girls selling something worth several hundred thousand, no several million yen for birdseed are such fools.' The girls aren't just undervaluing their bodies. They lowered the price on their own souls."

"They don't go as far as to sell their hearts. Girls like that say that it's a business where they just sell their bodies."

"They're just telling themselves that. Sure, they won't open their hearts as well to some old dude. But so what? Do you think the men are moved by that? When they make love to such girls, those guys are thinking, 'I bet this chick hates having sex with me so much that she could die. But what do I care? I've paid for what I've paid for.' In other words, by paying for it, they think they've earned the right to ignore the girl's feelings. How is that not devaluing your soul?"

Maybe it was because I rattled on like a machine gun or because she didn't really understand, but Juri fell silent with her head bowed. I heaved a sigh.

"There's stuff in the world that's worth more than money. I think that's people's hearts and time. You can't move someone's heart with money, and lost time can't be bought back with money. So if it'll help even a little with either of those things, I try not to be stingy." I pulled a page from my notebook and handed it to her. "Well, so much for our chat, we have to continue with our plan. Like I said, time is more valuable than money."

"What is this?"

"If you read it you'll know."

After Juri finished reading the note, she slowly raised her head. Her cheeks had stiffened. "We're making a call from here? I'm making it?"

"That's right. They want to make sure you're safe, and if they got a call from you, they'd be satisfied."

"Why from here?"

"Two reasons. One is in case they trace it. The other is those ships. I don't know what kind of recorder they've planted, but if it picks up that sound, we're in luck. The police will probably try to analyze it. If they figure out it's a ship's whistle, they're bound to presume that the hideout is located near the sea. They might even identify the whistles as being from Yokosuka's naval port."

"Basically, you're trying to mess up the investigation."

"You got it."

I pressed several buttons on the phone next to the bed. Soon my cell started ringing. After looking at its screen, I hung up the hotel phone.

"What are you doing?"

"I checked whether there's caller ID. It's okay, we can call as is." I pushed the phone toward Juri.

She folded her arms and stared at it, then licked her lips and lifted her face. "It might not be Papa who answers."

"I think it'll definitely be him, but if it's someone else, just ask them to get Mr. Katsuragi. However, only wait for ten seconds. Tell them that, too. When ten seconds pass, you hang up."

"I'm sure Papa will have a lot of questions."

"Probably. But there's no time for small talk. Say you can't answer questions and only say what's written on there."

"I got it." Juri slowly blinked once. "I'll try," she said, opening her eyes again.

I indicated the phone with my hand. Juri swallowed. She took a deep breath and reached for the receiver.

Her shaking fingertips pressed the buttons. As expected, my heart started beating faster. I kept asking myself if I'd missed anything.

The sound of the ringing escaped from between the receiver and Juri's ear. There were three rings. Then it connected. Someone's voice. But I couldn't tell whether it was Katsutoshi Katsuragi's.

"Oh, Papa? It's me. Can you tell from my voice? It's Juri," she said, looking at the note I'd written.

Even I could hear the person on the other end unleashing a storm of words. Juri sucked in a breath with a look of consternation.

"I'm sorry. We don't have the time to talk. You understand, right? Because I'm not alone. ...I can't answer that. Please just listen. We're running out of time."

I was staring at the clock's hand. It was already past fifteen seconds.

"I'm safe. So don't worry. They're saying they'll let me go home if they just get the money. ...Ah, I'm sorry. It looks like my time is up."

I rested my finger on the call button. Just as I thought I'd hang up in two seconds, I heard a distant whistle. I cut off the call immediately.

"Done!" I shook my fist and stood up. After closing the window, I turned to Juri. "Luck's on our side. That whistle went off at the perfect moment."

But Juri seemed off. Her back was hunched as though she felt cold.

"What's wrong?" I asked her, sitting next to her.

Her whole body was trembling. Just as I was about to ask her if she was okay, she clung to me.

"I've done it now, there's no going back," she murmured, pressing her cheek against my chest.

"Are you scared?"

Juri didn't answer. As I stayed still, I felt her trembling against my arm.

"It's natural," I said. "What we're doing isn't normal. It's something normal people are unable to do. But what we're getting in return isn't insignificant."

Juri nodded slightly and looked up at me. Her eyes were moist.

Unexpected feelings swelled inside of me. A certain impulse, you could say. Something that I hadn't noticed—or rather, that I'd noticed but had chosen to ignore—shook my heart.

I hugged Juri tighter. She looked at me with startled eyes.

Various thoughts crossed my head. Among them were a good number of self-serving takes. *Sleeping with this girl here wouldn't be such a big deal. In fact, deepening our relationship might be conducive to advancing the plan*—I thought that, too.

But I loosened my arms and moved away from her. What I wanted to do wasn't this. Right now, I was contending in the game of a lifetime.

"For now, let's leave. I don't think they traced the call, but nothing good will come from staying here for long."

Juri silently nodded.

We went back to the car, and I turned on the engine. When I was about to promptly depart, Juri said, "One sec." I stepped on the brake.

"I have a request," she continued.

"What is it?"

"There's a place nearby that I want to go to."

"Do you have something else you need to do?"

"It's not that, it's a place I like. Somewhere my mother who passed away took me once. Because I want to calm myself down… Please."

I saw Juri put her hands together and was taken aback a little. I didn't think the girl had it in her.

"Is it far?"

"I don't think it's that far."

"But I'd prefer to get as far away from this place as possible."

"Then it should be fine. It's not that close. I just meant it's not far by car."

"Hmm." I took my foot off the brake pedal. The car slowly

moved. "Do you know the way?"

"Yeah, I think."

I let out a sigh. "Then I'll leave the navigation to you."

"Got it. First, go back to the original road."

"Okay." I made a wide circle on the steering wheel and stepped on the accelerator.

I followed Juri's directions and continued down the highway. Soon, we got to a coastal road. On the left was the ocean, on the right were a chain of tall hills. After some time, Juri instructed me to turn right. As I turned the wheel and continued on, the road became steeper.

"We're going pretty high. Are you sure this is the way?"

"Yup," Juri answered confidently.

As I drove, the houses thinned out again. Nothing obstructed our view all around, and we could see the horizon more or less. Apparently we'd gotten up the hill and what followed was flat road.

"Stop around here."

Since Juri said so, I stepped on the brake. The place was pitch dark. It didn't seem like there were cars coming from either direction, but I parked on the roadside at least.

"Hey." Juri looked at me. "Could you open this?" She pointed to the roof.

"Here?"

"Because we're here."

I hesitated for a moment but eventually pressed the open switch for the hood. It quietly retracted. A chilly wind brushed my cheek. It was mixed with the smell of grass and soil.

"See? It's amazing." Juri looked up and pointed with her index finger.

Ohh, I let out a dumb gasp. The night sky was that beautiful. On the infinitely large, nearly jet-black display shone countless lights. Their positions were flawless. My heart was getting sucked in just from looking. "It's cliché but—"

Juri warned before I could finish, "Just don't say it looks like a planetarium."

I grinned, still looking up. She was right, I should stay away from that simile. "I don't know much about constellations. I'm regretting it."

"I just know Orion, pretty much. But that doesn't matter." She raised both her arms, stretched, and breathed deeply. "This feels great. It feels like it's not Japan."

I looked at our surroundings anew. The hills and valley were submerged in darkness. There seemed to be fields spread out in front of me.

"I wonder which way the ocean is," the words slipped out of my mouth though I didn't particularly need to know.

"That, that, and even that's the ocean." Juri pointed to three sides. "Because this is around the tip of the Miura Peninsula."

I nodded. The impressions I'd had as I'd driven agreed with what she said.

"Well, do you feel a little better?" I asked her.

"Yeah, thank you." Juri looked at me with a beaming smile. She blinked twice. "Is it okay if I ask you something?"

"What is it this time?"

"You tried to get closer to me back there, didn't you?"

For a moment, my breathing stopped. I averted my eyes from her and slowly breathed out. "You're the one who hugged me."

"That's not what I mean…" After pausing, she repeated, "You know that's not what I meant."

I didn't answer. I put my right hand on the steering wheel and fluttered my fingertips.

"Why did you stop? Because it'd be dangerous if we stayed there too long? In that case, would you have gone ahead if we did have the time?" she asked in a near whisper.

I hadn't seen these questions coming. "Then let me ask you." I turned to her, wearing a smile. "Why did you hug me? You might have gotten scared calling home, but I'm supposed to be nothing more than an accomplice to you."

She cast down her eyes before looking up at me again. "Because I decided to trust you. Because now that it's like this, I thought the only person I could trust was you."

The gleaming sincerity in her eyes confounded me. The tricky emotions that had threatened to sprout back at the love hotel were crawling into my heart again.

"Stockholm syndrome," I said.

Her lips opened as though to say, *Huh?* It was an incredibly childish expression that she hadn't shown until now.

"When a terrorist and hostage are together for a long time, supposedly a sense of solidarity will develop between them. Both parties do want the situation to be resolved quickly. It's a term for that state of mind. They mentioned it in a Bond movie."

"I'm not a hostage. You're not a terrorist."

"It's the same. You're isolated under abnormal circumstances. Even though it's staged, we're both hoping that the ransom exchange goes well, and that's just like the terrorist-hostage relationship."

Juri shook her head. "There's something that's completely different."

"What?"

"The solidarity that develops between the hostage and the terrorist is originally unnecessary, right? You can even say it's unnatural. But that's not the case for us."

I licked my lips and gave a small nod. "Certainly, our solidarity is a must."

"Right? So I wanted to feel it. My solidarity with you."

Juri's eyes caught me and wouldn't let go. I was growing weary of putting on the brakes. They even started to seem superfluous.

I drew her face closer with my left hand and our lips came together. Just before they did, she closed her eyes.

It's called flow. If you kiss, you want to put your tongue in. If the woman doesn't put up any resistance, you also want to touch her breasts, and if that continues, next you want to reach your hand into her underwear.

I wanted a change of venue but never got the chance to suggest it. Saying something like that could cool her passion. While I indulged in her lips, I thought this was a case of the syndrome after all. The act of calling home and talking to her father had wrecked something in Juri. As a result she was feeling hopelessly anxious. She couldn't deal with it without telling herself that she needed the man who was with her.

Well, what about me? Did I love the girl? No, that would have been stupid. It wasn't why I'd become interested in Juri, and my motive for staying with her belonged to a completely different dimension. I felt a very natural sexual desire simply because she was a young woman. I knew pursuing that was foolish, so I hadn't let it show in my behavior, and I still didn't mean to succumb to the impulse entirely.

But things turning out this way wasn't something that I could never welcome. I needed to dispel my anxiety no less than she did. Completing a game as big as this required absolute trust. For a man and woman to establish that, a physical connection was perhaps essential. It could even be an illusion, actually. It didn't matter if the emotions were momentary or false. Stockholm syndrome was precisely such a phenomenon.

When Juri brought out a condom from somewhere, I was fairly flabbergasted. It seemed she had brought it from the love hotel, but that meant she'd been expecting this to happen. I had to wonder if having a physical relationship was a standard way of establishing solidarity for her.

Inside the cramped car, we brought our bodies together and stimulated each other's membranes. To me, Juri seemed accustomed to sex. She also seemed to know how to enjoy it, too.

After the act, Juri said she was throwing out the trash and got out of the car. She didn't come back right away, so I put on my pants, too, and opened the door.

She was lingering at a spot not too far away. I called out to her back, "What are you doing?"

"Oh, nothing. I was just looking at the scenery a little."

I looked where she was facing. I could faintly see the ocean.

When I moved my line of sight to the foreground, it entered my vision. I had to laugh.

"What is it?"

"Look. There's a *jizo* right there."

She turned around and recognized the small stone Buddhist statue and its miniature shed. "You're right. I didn't notice."

"And you just said it feels like it's not Japan."

"Yeah." Juri's eyes were smiling, and she hugged my arm. "I feel a little cold. Let's go home."

"Sure," I agreed and kissed her one more time.

9

By the time we got back to the condo, it was nearly three a.m. In one night we had made a round trip to Yokosuka, had Juri make a phone call, and had car sex as a bonus. It was no wonder my body was tired, but oddly I didn't feel sleepy. Fortunately tomorrow was Saturday. When my focus had been on the automobile park plans, holidays weren't relevant, but now I didn't have any work to go in to the office for.

I booted my computer and visited the CPT website. Sure enough, there was a new post on the bulletin board.

I confirmed the quality of the product (Julie)
    Excuse me again, I'm the newbie Julie.
    Maniac, thank you for your valuable advice. Just earli-er, I checked it. It seems there's no problem with the CPT's quality.
    The agreement is next, at last. But I haven't been able to prepare the money and am in trouble. The banks are closed tomorrow so it might take some more time. Plus, I still don't know exactly how I'll be paying.

It seemed Maniac was the handle of some helpful person who didn't know the true meaning of the posts and had given Julie advice. Whoever it was had to be wondering how Julie had checked the car's quality in the middle of the night and scratching his head after seeing this message.

"Imagining Mr. Katsuragi's face as he writes these is kind of hilarious." Having said that, I thought it might actually be the detectives.

"So he'll go through with the deal because he confirmed I was okay," Juri observed, peeking at the screen from behind me.

"Well, I wonder about that."

"Uh, but..."

"He's saying that he needs some time to prepare the money. They're still trying to buy time. That's why they're demanding to know the method of exchange. Anyway, those guys are trying to coax us into making a move. Through that, they think they can grab us by the tail."

"Telling them the exchange method comes after they prepare the money, I guess?"

"Yeah, that's my thinking." I left the computer and sat down on the living room sofa. Juri followed me.

I turned over my thoughts. They were about what our opponents were up to. They couldn't just be lying in wait for us to make our move.

"Hey." Juri sat down next to me. "How are we getting the money? Do you have some neat idea?"

"Oh...yeah," I said ambiguously. If I told her I had no idea, what sort of face would she make? I couldn't afford to lose her trust at this point.

In fact, I was assuming that it would all work out. Outwitting the police wasn't so hard. They say kidnappings never work, but my hunch was that it wasn't true and that successful cases simply go unreported. The police were neatly hiding them to save face. Just the cases where the perp was caught were widely reported so that kidnappers always appeared to be dumb even from an amateur perspective. There had to be some in the world who were smart. The families, too, probably didn't want to complicate things once their precious child had come home. Spilling to the press and earning the culprit's grudge would do them no good.

"You're not going to tell me? How the exchange will happen?"

"I'll tell you in time."

"Are you trying not to make me feel agitated? You think I'd be scared? I'm not that weak."

"I don't think that—" I said with a wry smile. At that moment, I came up with something. Agitated… It wasn't a bad idea.

Nodding, I stood up. I went to the kitchen, took two cans of beer from the fridge, and came back to the sofa. I put one in front of Juri.

"What are you grinning about? It's creepy," she complained.

"I just thought of something fun. Those guys are going to get agitated."

"Agitated?"

"I'm going to tell them how the exchange will happen."

Juri was about to pop open her beer, but her hand froze at my words. "Are you sure about that?"

"You'll see. I won't just be showing my hand."

I returned to the computer and connected to the internet again. I performed several operations and accessed the site with the free email service. In the daytime, I had acquired an account there. The name and address were of course fake.

I opened a new mail window. Next, I took out my notebook and punched an address into the *to* field. It was the one of the person posting as "Julie" on the bulletin board.

"Well then." I put my hands on the keyboard and took a deep breath.

We are confirming that we received your message. We

are extremely delighted that you've learned that Juri Katsuragi is safe. Now we just need to move along the business negotiations. Letting this stagnate because of things that don't matter is just a drawback for both parties. We need to expedite this.

First, we would like you to prepare three hundred million yen as we told you. Please have it all in old ten-thousand-yen bills. Divide that in half and pack it in a caddy bag and in another bag.

Next, a cellphone. It can be the one you normally use.

When the above preparations are complete, notify us in the usual way. At that time, provide your cellphone number. You probably can't just write it out so you may apply some camouflage.

We pray that you complete the preparations quickly. Juri Katsuragi's prompt release will be tied to that.

We will tell you this just in case. There is no point in replying to this account. We will no longer use this address or look at emails sent to this address. It is only for this one-time occasion.

After reading it three times over, I sat up straight and carefully tapped the send button. In a few seconds, a notice that the email had gone out flashed on the screen. I immediately logged out.

"A caddy bag and a bag, huh. I see," Juri, who was watching from behind me, admired. "Because carrying that around isn't strange."

"Our opponents would think so, too."

I glanced sideways at Juri, who tilted her head quizzically, and drank my beer.

When would they notice the email? Soon, no doubt. They had to be checking regularly. Maybe the Katsuragi estate was in an uproar right around now.

I was dying to take a peek at the CPT Owners Club website but decided not to anymore for tonight. Being antsy wouldn't do me any good. Anyway, the other party was in a strategy meeting. I cut the internet connection and turned off the computer too.

The sound of the fan died down, and the room quieted to a surprising degree. I only heard Juri's breathing.

"We're done with the game for tonight. Good work."

"We'll finally get that ransom money." Her chest heaved. "You won't tell me how yet?"

"You'll know eventually," I replied with a smile. I wanted to tell her what I was up to, but she didn't need to know everything. "Let's go to sleep for tonight."

I had Juri sleep in the bed while I lay down on the sofa. She seemed a little dubious about that but didn't confront me.

To be frank, I was regretting having slept with her. It wasn't for any reason I could put my finger on. It might've been because I'd committed a prohibited move in the game. Or was it guilt, for having touched my precious "merchandise"?

That wasn't it.

Some kind of alarm was ringing in me as though to say, *You can't take it back now, can you?* It was a feeling you could only call intuition.

I didn't sleep well, probably thanks to that. Only having dozed off a little, I rose at pretty much my usual time. After washing my face in the bathroom, I booted the computer, also by force of habit.

I checked my email before hopping over to the CPT Owners Club. I glanced at the bulletin board and caught my breath.

Ready (Julie)
 Good morning. This is Julie. I've finally gotten the money. With this, I should be able to get the dear car I've been hoping for. All that's left is waiting for them to contact me.

By the way, these days, we can choose our plate numbers, yes?

I'd love to pick either:

3XXX or 8XXX

I've just started playing golf, so I can't wait for the day when I can put my golf bag in the trunk and drive.

10

I phoned in to Hotel Gardens and told them I wanted to make a reservation for tonight. I was transferred to the front desk and a male hotelkeeper came on the line. He asked how many people were staying, and I told him it was just me.

"Yes, we can prepare a single room for tonight."

"If possible, I would like a room facing the avenue."

"Do you mean on the front side?"

"I guess. And if possible, not too high up."

"Please wait a moment."

I was put on hold for about twenty seconds before the hotelkeeper's voice came back on.

"Thank you. Would a room on the fifteenth floor be fine?"

"The fifteenth floor. Sounds good, I'll have that room then."

"Certainly. May I have your name and phone number?"

I told him a bogus name and number, then hung up.

"What hotel?" Juri asked me without getting up from the sofa.

"Gardens. It's nearby. It's a pretty decent hotel. The crab egg shark fin soup at the Chinese restaurant in there is a delicacy. Apparently, the head French chef is the most medaled old man in Japan."

Juri had started shaking her head even as I spoke. "I'm asking you why you made a hotel reservation. It can't be to have a meal at their restaurant. Or are we moving to a new hideout?"

"We don't need a new hideout. We're just using the hotel for to-day."

"Are you using it for the ransom exchange?"

My shoulders shook with laughter. "I'm doing no such thing."

"Then what's the plan? What are you using it for? Just how are you going to do the exchange, anyway?" Juri demanded hysterically.

"Am I being interrogated or what?"

"But you won't tell me anything. Aren't we partners?"

"When the time comes, I'll tell you."

"Right now isn't the time? Papa gave his answer on the internet, didn't he? They've finished preparing the money. They also provided a phone number. The only thing left is the exchange."

I sighed and blinked slowly. "Like I said, this is a once in a life-time game. It won't progress that easily. If we don't go step by step, we won't get to the goal. This is just another procedure."

"But you told them to prepare the money... To pack it in a golf bag..."

"A necessary item to get to the next stage. You play videogames, don't you?"

"I haven't ever."

"Really? Anyway, for now just be quiet and watch."

She probably wasn't convinced, but nodded begrudgingly.

After finishing brunch, which was the cream stew that Juri had made the night before, I started getting ready to go out. I took a sports bag out of the closet, put a video camera and tape and a tripod into it, then binoculars and such. The binoculars were a gift from a bird-watcher friend of mine.

"You got a reservation for a single room, so I guess you're going to stay by yourself?"

"Today is Saturday, okay? Do you think a double room would be available? Even if one were, I wouldn't be able to specify the location or floor."

"So I can come with you?"

"Be careful not to be noticed by the hotel, though. Also, wear a disguise that won't look unnatural."

Juri stood in front of me and looked down at me with her hands on her hips.

"What?" I asked her.

"Don't 'what' me. How are you saying I should disguise myself? I don't have any clothes nor any makeup. I'd only be able to make myself look like a young homeless person."

Ha ha ha, I laughed. She had a way with words. "Then you'll wait in this room. The police must know what clothes you were wearing when you went missing. They've probably accounted for the chance that the kidnappers are using a hotel and circulated a notification."

"I'm going with you no matter what. I don't know what you're up to, but surely I can be of some help?"

I looked into her eyes. They said she wasn't backing down this time. I went over in my head what I would be doing soon. Having her there might prove convenient, in fact. I released my hand from the sports bag.

"Okay, okay. Let's go."

"I can come to the hotel, then?"

"First, we go shopping."

There's no kidnapper anywhere who would do this, I thought. I was going shopping at a department store in Ginza with the girl I'd kidnapped. In a way, I was doing what the police would never expect me to, but I couldn't keep very calm.

As though she couldn't care less about my state of mind, Juri rummaged through several racks of clothes. She looked no different at all from the other young women and beautifully melted into her surroundings, so it was hard to complain, but I wanted to tell her, *Think about why we've come shopping.*

At least she wasn't stupid, and she didn't make any blunders that would make the staff remember her face. Even as she looked for clothes, she deftly moved around. In fact, I might have been the one making an impression. I'd been standing in front of the window the whole time and watching her with a sour look. But if you thought of me as a man accompanying his young girlfriend's shopping despite himself, no director would order a retake.

Finally Juri came out of the store. She was carrying a paper bag.

"It seems you've somehow managed to buy something. I thought it'd take more time." I couldn't resist being sarcastic.

"This is the first time ever I've shopped so fast. The staff might remember me if I stayed at the store too long, so I chose stuff randomly."

"Remarkable, thanks."

"Then next is makeup. Let's go to the first floor." She sounded almost gleeful.

I waited in the tea lounge drinking coffee while Juri finished choosing. I wasn't sure about leaving her alone, but it wasn't like my presence would help. I had to take her word that compared to Shibuya, the chances of her running into someone she knew in Ginza were zero.

After about half an hour, she came back. When I saw her face, my eyes opened wide.

"You did your makeup?"

"Well, yeah, while I was at it," she said, sitting down across from me. The waitress came, so Juri ordered milk tea.

"You didn't have the staff do your makeup, did you?"

"Why would I? I just borrowed a mirror and did it myself. It's okay. In a place like that, no one's looking at other people. Everyone's just concerned with the face reflected in the mirror in front of them."

"Give me a break. I'm already worried as it is that they saw your face at the convenience store and the family restaurant."

"I'm saying it's okay." She took her cigarettes out of her handbag, but noticing the seats were non-smoking, returned the pack with an irritated look.

The milk tea came. I watched her face casually as she brought the cup to her mouth. Her makeup wasn't very thick and leveraged the fine texture of her skin. She had underscored her well-formed eyes and nose, and her face looked more vivid than before.

"What are you staring at me for? Are you still worried?"

"No, not really." I averted my eyes. "I have another item to shop for."

"What is it this time?"

"It's necessary for the game."

We got in another taxi and I directed it to Akihabara. In the car, I handed Juri five ten-thousand-yen bills.

"What's this?"

"Cash for shopping. Go and buy it for me."

"Well, I don't even know what I'm buying."

"When the time comes, I'll tell you. Do as I say."

Juri became sulky again, but I didn't want the driver to hear.

We went down Showa Road and then got off. The place was crowded on Saturdays. It was convenient for us since we didn't want to be seen. Even so, Juri wore a hat that nearly covered her eyes.

I went into an alley, away from a street that was lined with famous electronics stores. There were still a great number of people, but the atmosphere was somehow different. Many of the stores were meant for enthusiasts.

My eyes immediately settled on a man. He was swarthy and bearded—an Iranian.

"Go to that man and ask him if he has a burner," I said in Juri's ear.

"A burner?"

"A burner phone. It's a cell with a fake name."

"Ah." She nodded. "I've heard of those."

"Any maker will do. I think fifty thousand should be enough. Pay upfront. After that, he'll tell you to come with him, so do as he says and follow him. I'll wait around here."

"You're not coming with me?"

"If he mistakes it for a police bust, that'll suck. I'm having you go buy it in the first place to avoid that. It might be a little scary, but try your best."

Juri looked anxious for a moment, but soon nodded firmly.

"Okay. I'll go." She started walking toward the man.

I watched from a distance as she talked to the Iranian. He didn't seem all that surprised that a young woman had come to him. It was rumored among some ladies that you could buy a burner here. A woman who'd actually done so had told me.

Just as I thought, they started walking. They turned at a corner. Juri didn't look around at me. Way to go.

The guy with the goods would be waiting in a car. It was so they could beat a hasty retreat if it looked like a bust.

After about fifteen minutes, Juri came back. I felt relieved.

"Mission complete," she said. She held up a small paper bag. "I even got a souvenir."

"A souvenir?"

"A telephone card. They said it's infinite. It has fifty points right now, but once it gets to zero, apparently it resets."

I chuckled. "Like you'd ever use a public phone."

"Well, I don't have a cellphone right now." Juri fluttered the card in the air.

Juiced telephone cards must have been the Iranian gentlemen's main product line until recently. But with the spread of cellphones, the cards stopped selling, so they'd settled on burner phones as a replacement.

"Those guys' Japanese is good," Juri marveled. "I wonder how they learn it."

"People get serious when they need to survive. The same goes for whoever juiced that telephone card. Desperation. The NTT corporation isn't so desperate, so it'll be had every time."

"So to bust them, the police will have to get serious and learn their language."

"That's how it is."

I abruptly stopped walking. Juri, who had been clinging to my arm, pitched forward.

"What? Don't stop suddenly."

"I thought of a good way." I grinned. "Our game begins."

We went back to the condo by taxi, and I resumed our preparations. When I finally put my laptop in my bag, I was ready.

"I'll be calling you. I might sound like a broken record, but don't ever enter the hotel through the front."

"Enough, I know."

I was being persistent because I had my doubts, but I refrained from saying so and left. My wristwatch was pointing to three in the afternoon.

I took a cab and arrived at Hotel Gardens in just a few minutes. I got out at the front entrance and headed to the front desk. I was wearing a shirt and necktie under a dark gray suit. I was pretending to be a businessman who'd given up his weekend to come to Tokyo. In fact, the fake number I'd given had a Nagoya area code.

I wrote my fake name and fake address along with it on the lodging card, deposited fifty thousand yen, and finished the check-in formalities. The person at the front desk was looking down at the counter the whole time, but I did my best not to raise my face just in case.

My key card was for room number 1526. I declined having the bellboy guide me and went into the elevator.

When I got into the room, I immediately opened the window curtains. Diagonally to the lower left, I could see the Hakozaki Metropolitan Expressway Junction. I took the binoculars out from the bag and quickly focused them. A dark blue domestic car coming from the Ginza district went by within my field of vision.

First test cleared. I breathed out in relief. I'd stayed at this hotel once in the past and knew that I could see the junction. Naturally, at that time, I hadn't thought of any use for the view.

I took the phone and called home. It rang three times, and the answering machine message came on. I waited for the tone and opened my mouth.

"It's room 1526. When you come in, knock." Saying just that, I hung up. Juri would hear the message and immediately get going. I'd told her to use a taxi but to get off at Suitengu-mae on the Hanzomon subway line. From there, she could go underground and enter the hotel that way. Its B2 level was linked to the subway station. She could even use the elevator to go directly to the guest floors. In other words, she could completely bypass the front desk and lobby where people tended to be.

I took off my jacket, removed my tie, and started on the next part. I put the video camera on the tripod and set it at the window. Staring at the LCD screen, I adjusted the camera's angle and zoom. Now it could capture all of the cars coming from the Ginza district.

Then I took out my laptop. Using a cord I'd brought, I connected it to the jack by the desk. To comply with the needs of businessmen, in addition to the internal phone, the hotel offered a normal line that could connect to the internet. That was also something I had found out on my previous visit.

I booted my laptop and tried to access the internet, and it worked right away. Just in case, I went to the CPT Owners Club. There was a new message from "Julie."

Can't wait (Julie)

Even though I've made my offer and prepared the money, I haven't heard anything from them.

I wonder what they're doing. Hurry up and give me what's mine.

The golf caddy bag is crying at the door to be taken out.

Once again, I had to admire the incredibly well camouflaged writing. Anyone reading just this would surely think it was a girl who was bitching about not getting her car.

Anyway, that they were becoming impatient was evident. They couldn't wait to find out what hand the kidnappers would play.

I took a bottle of mineral water out of the fridge and drank directly from it. I went over the plan again. I was certain that I'd omitted nothing and that there weren't any holes in it.

I looked at the clock. Over thirty minutes had passed since I'd called. What was Juri doing?

Then, after another half-hour, there was finally a knock at the door.

"Who is it?" I asked just in case.

"Me," was the reply I heard. I opened the door.

"What in the world were you doing? If you were just changing clothes—" After getting that far, I fell silent. Juri's hair had turned brown, a brown that was almost blond. On top of that, it was shorter.

Heheh, she giggled. She quickly brushed up her hair.

"What the hell?"

"I dyed it. Not bad, right?" She looked around to appraise the room and approached the window. She looked into the video camera. "What are you filming?" she asked.

I wasn't the one who ought to be answering questions. "What are you thinking?" I demanded.

"Huh?"

"That hair. You don't think something as eye-catching as that is dangerous?"

"This? Eye-catching?"

"Look in the mirror."

"You told me to disguise myself, so I tried my very best. I cut my hair on my own, dyed it myself. I also slipped into my new clothes, so look. Don't I seem like a totally different person to you?" Her top was sleeveless and red, her bottoms were a black skirt. I was surprised that she had even changed her accessories and shoes. When had she bought them?

"I told you to wear a disguise that wouldn't be eye-catching."

Whether or not she'd heard me, she sat down on the bed and bounced her body up and down like a child playing on a trampoline. She was smiling.

"Hey, are you really a pro ad planner? Making a fuss over just this much is weird. Because right now there are fewer girls with black hair."

"And why do they dye their hair? Is it so they wouldn't stand out? That's not it. It's to be noticed."

"Maybe at first, but now it's different. Now black hair is just unfashionable. They don't want to be that, so they dye their hair."

I shook my head. It wasn't the time to be discussing something so stupid. "Anyway, when you get home, change it back. You might have forgotten, but you're a hostage. It'd be bizarre for a hostage's hair color to change during the kidnapping."

"Umm, the kidnappers are funky? They dyed the hostage's hair for fun?"

"You'll stop joking soon enough." I took out the cellphone we had obtained at Akihabara and shoved it in front of her face. "There, the game begins. Call your papa's cell."

"Me?" As might be expected, Juri's face grew stern again.

"I was going to call, but since you're here, I don't need to. I want to make sure that my voice is heard by Katsutoshi Katsuragi as little as possible. Even though it's very unlikely that your dad would remember it."

"I call, then what do I say?"

"I've thought it out. Come here." I had her sit in front of the computer. Then, I operated the keyboard and displayed a certain document on screen. It was something I had written while I waited for her. The document was divided into several items.

I pointed at the first bit. "Start with this. When you tell him this, you can hang up right away."

Juri stared at the sentences with an earnest look. Seeing her face, I realized that it had all been a pose. Being strangely bold as she shopped and dying her hair were merely the flip side of her anxiety.

"Is it going to be okay calling from this phone?"

"Make it as brief as possible. If you take too much time, they'll be able to specify the area."

She took a deep breath. She looked at the buttons on the cellphone.

"Right now?"

"Right now. This is the number." I put a note with Katsutoshi Katsuragi's cellphone number in front of her. "If you don't do it fast, the sun will set."

"And it's bad if it sets?"

"That video camera isn't infrared, and the binoculars aren't night-vision scopes."

She seemed to take my meaning more or less and nodded wordlessly. With another deep breath, she passed the cellphone to her left hand and brought her right index finger toward the buttons. Looking at the note, she carefully pressed each number. After she finished dialing, she brought the phone to her ear and gently closed her eyes.

I could hear the rings, too. After two, the phone connected.

"Hello, it's me. Juri. Don't say anything, just listen to me." She recast her gaze on the laptop screen. "Ten minutes after this, leave the house. Please load the caddy bag and other bag into the trunk of a car. Papa, you should be the only person in the car. Get on the Metropolitan Expressway and head toward Mukojima Interchange. …Mukojima, MU-KO-JI-MA. If you can, follow the legal speeds as much as possible. Well, I'll contact you again. …Sorry, we don't have the time to talk."

She hung up and looked at me with plaintive eyes. Her cheeks were a little flushed. I gently kissed her half-open lips.

"Good job."

"Am I contacting him next time, too?"

"Well, basically, you communicate for me."

"Basically?"

"You'll understand soon."

I accessed the internet again on my laptop. The Japanese Public Highway Corporation had a website that streamed information in real time. I went there. On the LCD display, a map of the Metropolitan Expressway appeared. The routes were indicated by white lines, but colored yellow or red depending on the congestion level. Today it seemed to be moving along more than weekdays, but even so, there were dabs of color here and there.

I followed the course that I thought Katsutoshi Katsuragi would take. There didn't seem to be too much traffic for now, only a little red before and after Hakozaki Junction.

Alternating between looking at the clock and the map of the Metropolitan Expressway, I finished the bottle of water. I was horribly thirsty. Juri also started drinking a cola. Neither of us said a word. I refreshed the traffic information now and then, but there was no big change. Any would be due to an accident. *Just not that*, I prayed from the bottom of my heart.

I looked at the clock and snapped my fingers. "Juri, the phone."

With a tense expression, she took the cellphone in hand. "What should I do next?"

"Ask him his present location. That's all."

Juri nodded and made the call. "Hello, it's me. Where are you now? …Uh, Takebashi? You've just gotten past Takebashi."

I gave her an okay sign with my fingers. She hurriedly hung up.

"He said Takebashi."

"Okay."

I shifted my gaze to the map of the Metropolitan Expressway. It was clear from Takebashi Junction to Edobashi. He could probably go at forty miles per hour. Edobashi to Hakozaki was moderately congested. That was an issue. The timing. It was all about the timing. I could only trust my instincts.

I snapped my fingers again. "Call. Confirm his position."

Juri pressed the redial button. It seemed she connected immediately.

"Where are you now? …Almost at Edobashi?"

I stood up and gave her an okay sign. She hung up in a hurry.

I stood at the window and double-checked the position of the video camera. I beckoned Juri over.

"Call in one minute. Instruct him to exit at Hakozaki. After that, hand the phone to me."

"To you? You're talking to him?"

"Yes. From there I'll do the talking," I said, nodding.

Exactly one minute later, Juri made the call. Next to her, I took a gas canister out from the bag.

"Hello, it's me. Exit at Hakozaki. Uh, don't hang up," she added hastily and handed the cellphone over to me.

I waited one beat and took the phone. It ought to have been light but felt awfully heavy. My heart started racing.

I stood at the window and used one hand to put the cellphone to my ear; in the other hand I held the pair of binoculars. I had already started the video camera.

I saw a silver-gray Mercedes gliding down the slope. I couldn't make out the driver. I looked at Juri, who was peeking at the video camera monitor. She just nodded. It was Katsutoshi Katsuragi's car.

I put the gas canister up to my lips, sucked in the gas, and spouted in one go, "Stay on the expressway and get on the circling lane."

Juri, who was listening right next to me, turned to me dumbstruck. I couldn't blame her. I had abruptly let out a voice like Donald Duck's. I hadn't thought a helium-based toy that altered my voice would ever serve such a use as this. It was a party novelty I'd bought for some occasion or other.

Katsutoshi Katsuragi must have been stunned, too. "What did you say? Wasn't I supposed to go to Mukojima?"

I breathed in the gas before answering, "Drive in the circling lane."

"There's an entrance to the Ginza district on the right. I don't need to go in there?"

"Drive in the circling lane."

At that point, I hung up the phone and gave it back to Juri. I monitored Hakozaki Junction through my binoculars. A silver-gray Mercedes went past. Several passenger cars followed. There was also a truck. And a taxi.

The Mercedes appeared again. Hakozaki Junction formed a small ring. If you didn't take any of the exits to head to any district, you could just go round and round until your tank was empty.

After the Mercedes had appeared a third time, I gave my next instruction to Juri. With a surprised face, she pressed the cellphone's redial button.

"Hello, it's me. The deal is off. Go home and wait for the next contact. …I'm sorry. I don't know what's happening, either."

After hanging up, she glared at me. I was sitting on the bed.

"What the heck, why did you suddenly cancel the deal?"

"Suddenly? That was the plan all along."

"All along. You were going to cancel anyway?" Juri came to my side and looked down at me. "What was all that trouble for?"

"Just figuring out the police's moves."

I stood up and stopped the camera I had left running.

11

The screen displayed Hakozaki Junction. The silver-gray Mercedes kept driving past several times. Various other cars also drove through. However, the only car that was displayed more than once was Katsutoshi Katsuragi's car.

"That's weird. It really is only the Mercedes."

Leaving the hotel room as it was, we had returned to the condo. Checkout was the next morning and I intended to do it then. If we checked out this evening, it would probably be suspicious to the hotel.

Juri was getting frustrated. "What the heck is weird? Just tell me already."

"That the only car driving in the circling lane is the Mercedes is what's weird. There ought to be more."

"But there are. Trucks and taxis, there's a ton."

"Only once, though. The only car driving round and round in the circling lane is the Mercedes, there's not one car among the others doing that."

"That's natural. The only car Papa was driving was the Mercedes."

"But there should be a tail following that Mercedes. The police tail."

Juri's mouth half-opened. It seemed she'd finally understood my ploy.

"If there aren't at least two or three of the police's cars, even if they're not following immediately after the Mercedes, that's weird. If they don't do that, they can't instantly support him. But then, looking at this video, there aren't cars that look like one. What's going on?"

Juri tilted her head without answering, still looking at the screen. I didn't think she'd have an answer to offer.

"There are a few things I can think of," I said. "One is that for some reason or other, they didn't have a police tail. In that case, they would be using an even better tracking method. For instance, an investigator was hiding in the Mercedes."

"I wonder if there was one." Juri's face approached the screen.

"Let's check."

I chose an image from the video where the Mercedes' interior was depicted most clearly and expanded it. The image was rough, but outlines were visible.

"It doesn't look like there's anyone in the backseat," I noted.

"Might he have been hiding in the trunk?"

"That's unlikely. A caddy bag and another bag with three hundred million yen were packed in there. Even if one person could fit, it'd be meaningless if he couldn't move. It's exactly why I instructed them to load the two bags in the trunk."

Juri nodded, looking convinced. It seemed she had modified her opinion of me a bit.

"Hey, in books and movies, the police usually put a transmitter in the ransom, don't they? Maybe they did that this time."

"They may have deposited a transmitter," I agreed. "But I doubt they'd rely on just that. Normally, they would always put a tail on, too. Or they would be watching from somewhere."

"Maybe they were."

"Impossible. We instructed him to go to the Mukojima Interchange. Why would they think to watch Hakozaki Junction along the way?"

"I agree, but…what do you think, then?"

"I don't know, which is why I'm bothered by it. Where in the world could those police guys have hidden?" I lay down on the sofa.

In fact, there was one more thing I could think of. But it was so hard to believe, I couldn't let it out of my mouth. It was that the police hadn't made a move. In other words, Katsutoshi Katsuragi hadn't notified the authorities of the incident. In that case, it wasn't a mystery that only the Mercedes had come.

But was it possible? Of course, I couldn't say it wasn't. Even Katsutoshi Katsuragi was a father. Maybe he was thinking first and foremost of his daughter's life and obeying that instruction not to tell the police.

But, I shook my head. He wasn't that sort of man. He wouldn't succumb to a simple threat. He would try to outwit the kidnappers no matter what and save his daughter too. In order to do so, he needed the police's help. The police had to be acting in some way. As Katsutoshi Katsuragi went around Hakozaki Junction like a horse on a merry-go-round, they had to have been waiting with bated breath for the kidnappers to appear.

"Hey, so when is it?" Juri asked.

"When is what?"

"The real time we exchange me and the ransom. What else? Or are you still planning some dry run?" She stood beside me and spread her arms. Her tone was mocking. It seemed she didn't like my way of doing things.

"I just want to do it perfectly. That's for your sake, too. You want the money, don't you? You want revenge on the Katsuragis, don't you?"

"Yes. But I don't want to dawdle."

"We're not dawdling. We're just being careful. Because, after all, this is Katsutoshi Katsuragi."

"When are you doing it?"

"Why are you being so impatient? There's no need for haste. The ace of spades is in our hands. We'll choose the right time and obtain the money in a secure way."

Juri shook her head vigorously. Her shortly cropped hair went wild. "You might be having fun thinking of this as a game, but put yourself in my shoes, too. I don't want this tension anymore. I want to be able to relax."

Shouting those words, Juri rushed into the bedroom. Her reaction felt sudden to me. I understood her feelings, but I didn't see why a wave of emotion had surged forth now.

When I went into the bedroom, Juri was lying prone on the bed. I sat down next to her and stroked her recently dyed hair. She'd been so bold in showing me her 'do, so what was with this change?

Juri's hand came around to my back. I silently lay down on my side. Then my body covered hers.

"Hug me tight," she murmured. "The only time we can be together is now."

Indulging in sex was ridiculous. I understood that, but how had I come to think fondly of this girl who was using my armpit as a pillow?

The only time we can be together is now—that was true. After we successfully completed this game, we would never meet again. We couldn't do something so dangerous. That had been my intention since the beginning.

But it bugged me now. Frankly speaking, I was starting to want to extend my time with her. It wasn't just that. I was thinking of ways not to part with her even after scoring the ransom.

What's gotten into you, Shunsuke Sakuma? You weren't that kind of man.

The next morning when I woke up, Juri wasn't next to me.

Instead, the smell of coffee wafted through the air.

When I peeked from the bedroom doorway, Juri was going back and forth between the dining table and kitchen. There were already several dishes resting on top of the table.

I took the digital camera resting on the cabinet, and from the door's gap, aimed it at her. It was right when she was carrying a tray. I pressed the shutter, making sure the flash wouldn't go off. She didn't notice. When I checked on the camera display, it was somewhat dim, but she was captured beautifully. I opened the cover right there and took out the memory card.

"Are you up?"

Juri approached, apparently having heard me sneaking around. I quickly returned the camera to the cabinet. The card remained gripped in my hand.

The door opened and Juri came in. I was standing right next to the door, so she looked surprised.

"What, were you up?"

"I just woke up. It looks like you prepared breakfast for me."

"Because I'm a freeloader. I need to give back a little. And we'd get tired with just cream stew."

When Juri turned her back to me, I seized the chance and slipped the card into the inner pocket of a jacket hung up nearby.

Ham, eggs, vegetable soup, toast, and coffee made up the menu. It wasn't what you'd call cooking, but considering the contents of the refrigerator, she couldn't have done any better.

"It's like I'm a married man," I tried and mumbled the words after taking a bite of toast.

"Why aren't you married?"

"Well. Me, I want to know why people do get married. I can't possibly swear to spend my entire life with someone I'm bound to get sick of."

"But that person, at least, will stay by your side. No matter how ugly of an old man you become, you won't be alone."

"In exchange, no matter how ugly of an old woman she becomes, I have to stay by her side. And sooner or later, you're alone. Whether you're married or not, it's the same."

"But wouldn't you have your kids? Even if your spouse passes away, your family would still be there."

"Is that right? Look at me," I pointed at my chest with my fork. "I have parents. But I'm living alone like this. I haven't called them in years. Is a son like that family to his parents? It's as good as not having me."

"Even if you're not home, they know you're somewhere. Maybe your parents are satisfied with just that. Maybe they enjoy just imagining the kind of life you're leading."

I snorted and brought the coffee to my mouth. She looked at me as if to say, *What's so funny about that?*

"I didn't think you'd be telling me about the importance of family."

Juri cast down her eyes. I'd poked her where it hurt.

I crushed the egg yolk and mixed it with the ham, then put it in my mouth.

"Why don't you talk to your parents?" she asked, still facing down.

"I have no business with them—that'd be the most accurate way to put it. They're just a nuisance to me. Sometimes I get a boring call about clerical stuff and once that bit is over, we have nothing left to discuss."

"Where's your family home?"

"It's in Yokohama. Around Motomachi."

"That's a nice area."

"Girls always say that. Walking around there on your boyfriend's arm and being born and raised there are different things."

"Do they have some kind of store?"

"My father was an ordinary white-collar worker. Nothing to do with the Motomachi shopping street at all."

"Is your father still working?"

I shook my head. "Actually, he died. When I was in elementary school."

"Oh...I see."

"My parents got divorced. I was taken in by my father. But he died of illness so I was returned to my mother. At the time she was back at her family's house, so I lived with them."

That household ran a furniture store. It was a pretty famous store locally. My grandfather and grandmother were in good health and living with their oldest son's family. So my mother and I had joined them. My mom helped with the shop and also handled the housework. I never felt unwanted there at the house my mother had been raised in. It wasn't just my grandparents who were affectionate toward me, but also the eldest son and his wife. They had a daughter and son, and neither treated me like a freeloader.

"But I noticed eventually. It was a manufactured peace."

"What do you mean?"

"In the end, my mom and I were just a nuisance for them. Of course we were. A divorced woman with a child living with them indefinitely, family or not, was a nuisance. In particular, I wasn't related by blood to my aunt, so no wonder she was annoyed. She didn't show it clearly on the surface, but you sense that sort of thing. When I really watched her, though, I saw that we weren't the only ones she was two-faced with. My aunt was a rock-solid person who was also a gifted businesswoman. The one managing that store wasn't really my uncle but my aunt. The employees trusted her more, too. That made her confident. She didn't just stay behind the scenes and bossed around her husband and father-in-law. I don't think my grandparents found it amusing. They were trying to find a way to reinstate their wobbly son. But this uncle of mine was really worthless. If he came across a bothersome situation, he hid behind his wife. It must have been frustrating for my grandparents, but they'd retired. If their daughter-in-law was maintaining the store, even if they hated it, they had to be civil. Thanks to all that, various vibes swirled in that big family."

In concluding my lengthy response, I added, "Boring stuff."

"It's not boring. So then what did you do? I think it must have been hard being considerate among those kinds of adults."

"It wasn't hard. I was bewildered, but once you figure out how everything works, it's easy. The point is that I sensed there were rules. As long as I followed those rules, it wasn't difficult at all."

"Rules?"

"Everyone wore a mask to accommodate the situation. You couldn't do anything that would remove our masks. Reacting strongly to someone else's actions was pointless. After all, it was just a mask. So I decided to put on a mask, too."

"What kind of mask?"

"In a nutshell, the most appropriate mask for the situation. As a kid, it meant fulfilling adult expectations. Although that didn't simply mean being a good boy. When I was little, I wore the mask of a mischievous child; after some time, I wore the mask of a rebellious teen. After that, the mask of adolescence. The mask of a young man pondering his future. In any case, it had to be a mask that was familiar to adults."

"Unbelievable…"

"It was no big deal. And wearing a mask is just easier a lot of the time. No matter what anyone says, the other person is talking to a mask. I can just stick my tongue out under it, and in the meantime, I can think of what kind of mask to wear next to make them happy. Human relationships are cumbersome things. But by adopting this method, it becomes nothing."

"You've been doing that ever since?"

"I've been doing that ever since."

Juri put her fork down and hid both her hands under the table. "It seems kind of lonely."

"Does it? I don't think so. To begin with, everyone wears a mask to some degree in going about their lives. Hasn't that been true for you, too?"

"I wonder..."

"It's an unlivable world otherwise. If you expose your true face, you don't know when it'll get pummeled. This world is a game. It's a game where, depending on the situation, you put on the relevant mask."

"The mask of youth, huh."

"What did you say?" I pulled back my fingers from my coffee cup. "What did you just say?"

"Nothing."

"No, I know I heard it. The mask of youth... Why do you know the name of that game? It hasn't come out yet."

I glared at her. After averting her gaze for a moment, she looked up fearfully. The pink of her tongue peeked out between her lips.

"I'm sorry. I looked."

"At what?"

"At the stuff lying around. The stuff on your computer."

I sighed and put my fingers around my cup. I sipped some coffee. "Did I not tell you not to touch my stuff?"

"That's why I'm apologizing. But you have to understand. I wanted to know more about you. What kind of person you are. And how you were born and raised."

"Everything to know about me, I just told you. I wasn't really happy, and I wasn't especially miserable."

"Your mom right now?"

"She remarried when I was in high school. He's a company man who deals with construction materials. He's a quiet person, and he was kind to me—" I shook my head and corrected myself. "He wore the mask of a kind man, is what I should say. And he's probably continuing to wear it now.

"That's all there is to say about me," I concluded. Juri didn't ask anything more. I regretted drawing out my reminiscences.

After breakfast, I returned to the CPT Owners Club on the internet. There was a new post there.

24 hours (Julie)

Good morning. Even though I prepared the money, suddenly the agreement got postponed. Boo. I'm kind of pissed off, so I've decided to put a 24-hour time limit on it. If they don't contact me by then, I just might to have to go to you-know-whom!

Sorry for bitching so early in the day.

12

Juri's hair when she got out of the bathroom was a dark maroon. It seemed a little brighter than her original color, but it was better than the earlier blond.

"That looks better on you," I said. "Blond hair doesn't suit Japanese people."

"Adults all say that."

"Aren't you an adult?"

"I mean older men."

"When I see Japanese people with flat faces and blond hair, I'm embarrassed for them. It's like they're showing off a Western complex." Seeing she was becoming angry, I added, "I'm talking about young people in general. I wasn't saying your face is flat. Of course, it's not carved as deeply as a Caucasian's."

Maybe thanks to the last unnecessary bit, she brusquely sat down on the sofa looking no less peeved. "So did you think of a good method?"

"I'm thinking."

"You're still thinking? We only have twenty-four hours now." She looked at the clock and shook her head. "Since that post was written at six in the morning, if we have until tomorrow at six that's seventeen hours."

"There's no need to dwell on that."

"But if he isn't contacted by then, he says he'll go to the police…"

I raised one hand to stop her from talking and then picked up the stereo remote. When I started the CD, it was midway through *The Phantom of the Opera*. I loved the musical and had seen it several times. It was the story of a sad man who covered his hideous figure with a mask to become something more than human.

It isn't just him who's wearing a mask—that was my impression every time.

I just might have to go to you-know-whom. What did that mean? Did it mean he would contact the police? Ridiculous—as in, he hadn't contacted them yet? If he thought a threat like that would work, then he wasn't taking the kidnappers seriously.

And yet I couldn't be entirely sure. According to my own Hakozaki Junction operation, the police weren't involved.

Maybe Katsutoshi Katsuragi really hadn't gone to the police yet.

I shook my head. There was no way. It was a trap. They were giving us the illusion that the police weren't on the case just so we'd act recklessly.

"You should have gotten it yesterday while he was doing that," Juri said.

"Doing what?"

"Driving in circles in Hakozaki. You saw that he didn't have a police tail. So we could have just had him leave his car there. Once Papa left, we could have moved the money from the car or even driven away in it."

"How stupid. The police would have followed us immediately."

"Where were they? There weren't any."

"It's not that there weren't any. They had to have been watching the Mercedes from somewhere."

I thought they might have been standing by at various interchanges on the Metropolitan Expressway. I also needed to assume that they'd listened in on our exchanges with Katsutoshi Katsuragi.

"Say we told them to bring the ransom to a designated place," I said. "We could tell the person who'd brought the cash to leave immediately. But if we nonchalantly went to get the ransom, we'd get caught no matter what. Do you know why?"

"Because the police are watching."

"Right. The detectives would have their eyes peeled waiting for the culprit to appear. They say that's the best moment to nab a kidnapper. Then I'll ask this: how do the police know about the place?"

"That's obvious. It's because the hostage's parents or someone tells them."

"Exactly. In other words, not telling them the exchange location until the last minute is only prudent. But if you don't tell them anything, the person who's transporting the cash doesn't know where to go. It's a difficult tradeoff."

"So you indicate the general location. Then, once they get close, you tell them the exact spot."

"You say it like it's easy, but that usually doesn't go well. You should assume that the police's network will react quickly. It's not even a matter of minutes. You have to carry the thing out in seconds."

"And you're thinking how."

"Well, yeah. It's taking shape, though. I'm glad I took my studies seriously."

"Your studies?"

"You'll see."

I booted the computer and, after massaging my fingers, wrote the following text:

Dear Katsutoshi Katsuragi,

Due to an unexpected development yesterday, we were forced to suspend plans. The unexpected development was the involvement of the police. While we observed, we felt their presence. While it is unclear whether or not we were right, if you did contact the authorities, and if some sort of investigation has been opened, that is extremely regrettable. We would need to drop this deal immediately. Juri Katsuragi would never be able to return to you.

We will warn you once more. Do not have the police intervene. If in the next transaction, we feel they have, we will withdraw without hesitation. We will not contact you. And there will be no exchange after that.

In other words, for both of us, this is the last chance. Now we will give you several instructions. We do not want to meet further unexpected difficulties.

- Fit the three hundred million yen ransom into as small of a bag as possible. We would think a suitcase would be reasonable. You do not need to lock it with a key, but wrap the bills in a black plastic bag so that the contents are not distinguishable by just opening the top. You may by no means deposit a transmitter. If there is evidence of one, we will consider that a breach of our agreement. We have prepared a means of checking for a transmitter.
- Prepare a notepad, writing utensils, and cellophane tape.
- The transporter this time is your wife. The transport vehicle will be your wife's BMW. Like with the ransom, you may not have a transmitter on your wife or the car. If we detect any, the deal will be off.
- Prepare a cellphone for your wife. Provide the number on the usual website.

Our next contact will come within twenty-four hours. Be on standby.

After reading it four times over, I used an account made with a fictitious name and sent it. Now, there really was no turning back.

"Do you have a way of checking for a transmitter?" Juri asked.

"There are several methods. A metal detector would work, or even a radio wave detector."

"But then, you can't use those until you have the ransom in hand."

I smirked. "True."

"Then why give out those instructions? Isn't it pointless?"

"It'll be somewhat of a deterrence. You could call it a threat. They have no idea what methods we'll resort to, so they have to heed our warning."

"Are you sure they will?" Juri tilted her head.

"I think the ransom itself will probably not have a transmitter. Even if the exchange is successful, it could anger the culprit, which they don't want. If they do plant a transmitter, it'll be on the transporter or the car."

"So...on Mama or the BMW."

"Because of that, we need to first prepare a countermeasure. Of course, I've thought of one."

"Tell me."

"You have something to look forward to."

"That again?" Juri made a tired look and frowned. "Can you stop acting so smug? It's really off-putting. Don't you see me as a partner?"

"You're my only and best partner. Without you this next plan definitely won't be successful. Or rather, it won't be feasible. In a way, you'll have to hustle more than me."

My assurance of sorts seemed to improve her mood a bit. Her large eyes started glittering. At the same time, that light was colored with tension.

"What am I going to do?"

"You'll put on an act." I looked into her eyes. "It's a big role. A very big role."

The next day, Monday, I got out of bed following my routine. Although that didn't mean I had slept well. I was excited thinking about finally reaching the big act, and just as I thought I was dozing off, I'd suddenly wake, over and over again. My head was a little heavy.

I washed my face, and while I was doing my regular exercises, Juri called out from the bed.

"You're already awake?"

She seemed not to have slept well, either. Her eyes were red.

"Because I've got to go to work."

"Work? On a big day like this?"

"Because it's a big day. I can't do anything that's different from usual. On the chance they become suspicious later, it would be really bad if I took the day off."

"Do you think you'd be suspected?"

"That..." In my pushup position, I shook my head side to side. "...should be unlikely."

"In that case—"

"It's okay," I said. "Today is a Monday, no different from any other. So I'll head out like usual, go to meetings, and craft business proposals. I don't want to ruin that rhythm just for a game."

I couldn't tell whether she understood what I was saying, but Juri fell silent.

During breakfast, we made our last arrangements. I would go to work, but the plan would be executed after I came home. I didn't intend to do overtime today.

Tedious tasks awaited me when I got to the office. I had to attend a promo planning session for the idol talent. The strategy was to double her up with a game character, but it was something every company was doing and there was nothing novel about it. They had requested my opinion and when I said exactly that, the place was instantly subdued. The guy who was nudging the meeting along asked if I had any ideas, then.

"How about we gather several similar-looking girls," I threw out an idea that happened to pop into my head. "If you brought girls who were about the same build and had the same facial features and put makeup on them, they'll look even more like each other. Line up ten of them with the same face, but only one of them is real. Well, which? You don't enlighten them for a while. I think it'd become a hot subject."

It'd probably become a hot subject, but it wouldn't help sell the idol, someone opined. *It'd follow the pattern of a stunt and that'd be it.*

I didn't object. The man was right. But his thinking was wrong in that idols were just a stunt. However, I stayed silent because my views on such a job being accepted or not didn't matter.

When afternoon came, I secretly checked the internet. On the CPT Owners Club bulletin board, there was a new post from "Julie." The site's actual visitors were perhaps growing mistrustful of this new frequent poster.

Finally (Julie)

Hello. I heard back from my contact. They say this time they want to close the deal. They put in a whole bunch of conditions, even though I've been telling them that as long as I get my hands on the car I want, anything is all right. So anal. They made me wait so long that the number I want has changed!

Now it's 4XXX and 7XXX.

Aaah, I want to hurry up and sign already.

I noted the numbers written there. It was probably Katsuragi's wife's cellphone number. With this I had collected almost all the components.

When I cut my internet connection, I saw Kozuka approaching from the front. I switched the screen to a proposal.

"What's up?" Kozuka asked with a forced smile. It was his tell that he had bad news.

"I'm doing reasonably well. I'm getting fired up about my new project." I'd be happy if he heard it as sarcasm. I said it with that intent. Kozuka scratched his head.

"It seems you're not enthusiastic about the Yumi Kurihara promo."

He must have heard from the staff at the meeting. I could imagine the details of the slander. "That's not true. I'm trying my best to come up with ideas."

"The idea to have ten similar-looking people isn't bad, I agree."

I smiled with just my mouth. He was flattering me out of pity, and that made me feel more miserable than angry. Since when had I become such a loser?

"You're with me from three o'clock. I have a place I want you to visit with me."

"Where would that be?"

"Nissei Automobile HQ."

I stared back at Kozuka's face. He was avoiding eye contact. "That's strange, isn't it? They pushed me out of the team, but they keep summoning me. What's their deal?"

"To be honest, I don't know. The attendance request list had your name on it, and that's why I'm asking you."

"On whose whim, I wonder? Can't be Mr. Katsuragi's."

"Who knows. It seems Mr. Katsuragi will attend, too, so you can ask him."

"Mr. Katsuragi? You're kidding."

"No, there's no mistake—I assume. I just got the fax."

Even so, I couldn't help but think it was impossible. What was the man thinking? His daughter had been kidnapped, and with the ransom exchange looming, he had the nerve to casually attend a meeting? Or was he betting that it would take place earlier in the day than that anyway? *Even so*, I thought.

"What'll you do? If you don't want to, I won't make you. There's no problem with declining and saying that you have some other important business. They were the ones who pushed you off the team, after all."

"No, I'll come," I said. "Seeing Mr. Katsuragi's face wouldn't be bad."

I didn't know how he took those words, but Kozuka grinned and smacked me on the back.

When it was past three in the afternoon, I headed towards the Nissei Automobile Tokyo headquarters with Kozuka and several of the new car campaign staff. Sugimoto was ignoring me. He must've been thinking, *Why is this guy here?*

Traffic was light, so we arrived earlier than planned. Sugimoto and the others started preparing in the meeting room, but I didn't have anything to do. I left the room for a moment, bought instant coffee from the vending machine, and went to a smoking area that was lined with plants. Kozuka was there smoking a cigarette.

"Sugimoto and the others were saying that something's the matter with Nissei," he told me.

"Which means?"

"I guess you'd say it's directionless. It's losing focus, ever so subtly. It seems even the great Nissei is teetering thanks to the prolonged recession."

I silently nodded, but I thought it might not be just the recession. What may have been teetering was Katsutoshi Katsuragi's mental state.

THE NAME OF THE GAME IS A KIDNAPPING

When I was about to ask for specific examples, Kozuka trained his eyes behind me and his face stiffened. Just from that, I knew who was behind me. I turned around. Katsutoshi Katsuragi was standing there with one hand in his pocket.

13

"Sorry for bothering you at such a busy time." Katsutoshi Katsuragi approached us. He looked sharp in a dark blue double-breasted suit. His smile was relaxed, too.

"No, it's nothing at all." Kozuka remained standing at attention.

"I had several things I wanted to check on a plan from you that came up the other day. That's why I suddenly had you come."

"Then today's meeting is by your instruction?"

"Well, yes. I become restless when something catches my attention." Katsuragi looked at his wristwatch. "It's almost time. Shall we?"

"Excuse me, but I brought him, too." Kozuka looked at me.

Katsuragi faced me so I lowered my head. But then he immediately took his eyes off me. "What about him?" he asked Kozuka.

"No, there was an instruction in the document from your side that Sakuma should attend."

"Hmm." Katsuragi tilted his head. "I wonder why. I have no idea. The point person might have looked at an old list and automatically sent it. Well, it doesn't matter. Let's get to work," he said, then started walking ahead.

Kozuka spoke close to my ear. "What do you want to do?"

"What do you mean?"

"It seems that Mr. Katsuragi doesn't really have any business with you. Attending might just be unpleasant for you. You can just go back if you want."

I did feel like splitting, but I didn't say that out loud. "I came, so I'll at least listen. Even if I went back to the office, I don't have any big project."

No doubt hearing the poison in my voice, Kozuka nodded with a slightly irritated look.

I pretended to go to the bathroom and left Kozuka. I found a place with no prying eyes and took out my cellphone. I called Juri.

"Hello, what is it?" It might have been because she hadn't thought that she would be contacted this soon, but she sounded puzzled.

"Change of plans. We'll go through with it thirty minutes from now."

"In thirty minutes? Wait a second, don't tell me that suddenly."

"Whether we do it in thirty minutes or five hours, what you're doing won't change."

"I'm saying I need to prepare myself for it mentally."

"That's why I'm saying in thirty minutes. Finish preparing yourself mentally by then."

"Wait. What should I do about the last part? Should I do it like how we were saying? If they don't trust me, then what?"

"They'll trust you. There's no reason not to."

When I said so confidently, Juri relented. I heard a big sigh. "It's definitely going to be okay, right?"

"Don't worry. I haven't fumbled at this kind of game before."

"Okay. If you're that sure, I'm going to get ready. In thirty minutes."

"Yup."

"What are you going to do? You're at the office, aren't you?"

"I'm at your papa's company. I have a meeting coming up with him."

"Wha-"

"I'm leaving it all to you. All of this is hanging on your acting skills."

Haah—a huge sigh. "I got it. I'll try. But if it doesn't seem like it'll go well, I'll stop immediately."

"It's okay. It'll go well."

I hung up and headed to the room where, in thirty minutes, the man I would confront with a different game was waiting.

The meeting was about a project using an internet camera. They would equip one to the announced new car and drive it around town. Customers thinking of buying the car could use the internet to see that video. The video wouldn't merely show what lay beyond the windshield, but also the car's interior, the dashboard, each mirror, and so on—everything the driver could see would be captured. If they clicked with a mouse, they could freely change the camera. They would be able to take a test drive without leaving home, so to speak. It wasn't a bad idea, but it wasn't fundamentally different from what informational programs on new cars did. True, it was significantly cheaper than my automobile park project.

"There are limits to the transmission rate, so conveying velocity will be a challenge, I think. What will be very relevant is what street to drive on, and making the scene overseas will certainly increase the appeal, we think." It was just the staff from our company nodding at Sugimoto's explanation. Of course, I didn't nod.

Katsutoshi Katsuragi raised his hand. The tension rose instantly. "We're not trying to introduce our car on a late-night program."

I was slightly surprised by his remark. It seemed Katsuragi shared my impression.

"We don't want to just show a cool video. That's unnecessary. The information we want to communicate to buying customers is the new car's excellent cost performance. We don't want to make a buzz of it, we want to convey an accurate feeling of driving it. So it's meaningless if it's not a street that the general public needs to drive on. If you show them images of it driving through Australia or California, that's not helpful to the customers at all."

It was annoying, but I agreed with his opinion. When I peeked at Sugimoto and Kozuka, they were exchanging troubled looks. Perhaps they were going to make the location Australia.

I glanced at the clock. Since calling Juri, twenty-seven minutes had passed.

Then the seconds hand made three laps around the face of the clock. I examined Katsutoshi Katsuragi's expression. There was no apparent change in it. It looked as though he were focusing on this boring meeting.

Finally, that straight face clouded over in an instant. Katsuragi put his hand in the inner pocket of his suit. It was as I thought. The guy hadn't turned off his cellphone.

"Excuse me for a second," he said and exited the room.

The meeting was on hold. *The EVP leaving his seat to take a call is so unusual*, the guys from Nissei Auto were murmuring.

Soon, Katsuragi returned and whispered something into the ear of one of his subordinates. When the latter nodded, Katsuragi left the room again without saying a word to us.

"Um, Katsuragi has left on urgent business. However, he asked that we continue this meeting."

"But without Mr. Katsuragi, is there any point in going on?"

"We're familiar with his general position."

"Is that right." Kozuka put on a sour face, which was unusual. You couldn't blame him when the person who'd called the meeting had up and left.

I brought my face towards Kozuka. "President, I'm going back to the office. It seems that me being here for any longer is meaningless."

Kozuka nodded yes. He probably didn't have the time to be concerned about me.

When I left the room, I was seized by a desire to go to the parking lot. There was no mistaking that around now, Katsutoshi Katsuragi was hurriedly turning on his Mercedes' engine in the executive parking space. But then, having someone witness me watching him was too big of a risk. I decided to be patient and headed to the front entrance.

I hailed a taxi outside Nissei Automobile's headquarters and decided to return to Aoyama for the time being. However, near the office, I got off and immediately hailed a different taxi. I told the driver to head toward Asakusa. I looked at the clock.

Juri would first have called home. There, Katsuragi's wife had been on standby. What kinds of things had she said to Juri, who wasn't really her daughter? There were detectives next to her, so Mrs. Katsuragi might have at least spoken with a tone of worry. In her heart, she was surely cursing a development that was costing them three hundred million yen.

Juri would have instructed her to immediately load the money and depart. No details as to the destination—we'd decided that the instructions would be to 'head west on road X' and so on.

Juri had also called Katsutoshi Katsuragi. I was there. Her instructions to him were succinct: fetch a cardboard box and tape and be ready to leave in his Mercedes on a moment's notice.

I called Juri.

"Hello, it's me." Juri's voice sounded bubbly to me.

"How was it?"

"I did everything just like you said. Mama will get to Shinjuku soon."

"Good, next step then. I'm already heading there."

"Got it." She hung up.

Putting away my cellphone, I imagined Katsuragi's wife's BMW pulling up to City Hall. Juri would be calling Katsutoshi Katsuragi and giving him directions to head there too.

There would probably be a police tail on the BMW. And almost certainly, there was a transmitter or bug on the car or wife. What we had to do first was to remove those devices. In order to do that, we had to trade the driver and car.

On the next call Juri would instruct them to move the ransom from the suitcase to the cardboard box. Then, Katsutoshi Katsuragi would transport the cash in his Mercedes. With that, all the troublesome devices would be gone.

When I had told Juri this plan, she had frowned.

"Even if you change the car and driver, it's over if they just transfer the transmitter or bug."

I shook my head immediately. "They wouldn't do that."

"How do you know for sure?"

"Because they can't be seen doing it. Your parents aren't the police. There's no way they could secretly transfer the equipment without catching anyone's attention."

"But we won't be there."

"And how would they know that?"

"Oh...right."

"The culprits might be watching from somewhere—so long as we make them think so, the game continues to our advantage. You could say this is poker."

As my body swayed in the cab, I prayed for Juri to execute her several procedures successfully. Our opponents believed she was being made to call. That she was acting independently was probably something they wouldn't even dream of. That alone had the potency of a straight flush.

I got out of the taxi as we approached Komagata bridge. From here I would go on foot. I sorted through the plan in my head as I walked. *It's okay, it'll go well.*

A skyscraper stood facing the expressway. It was the building of a certain beer company. I took the elevator to the top floor. It had an observation deck that doubled as a beer hall. I bought a meal ticket for a draft beer at the entrance.

The place had a U-shaped counter with seats that faced the window. There were several guests. I settled down at the left corner. I took out my binoculars and focused them on the expressway. That wasn't unusual for the guests here, so no one paid any attention. Or rather, they weren't looking anywhere except out the window, and the staff could only see the guests' backs.

If Juri had done her work without a hitch, then Katsutoshi Katsuragi's Mercedes should already be heading this way. I was a little anxious. I needed Juri to be here soon, or I would be in trouble.

When I tried looking at my wristwatch, someone tapped my shoulder. Juri took a seat to my left. She was wearing an aqua dress.

"Mr. Katsuragi is…?" I asked in a whisper.

"Just now, he got on the expressway," Juri replied curtly.

I held up the binoculars. Although the lens had pretty high magnification, picking out Katsuragi's Mercedes from among the traffic was difficult.

"Call him. Confirm his location."

Juri did as she was told. It seemed the call went through right away.

"Hello, it's me. Where are you now?" she asked in a low voice. "What? You just got on the Mukojima segment?"

I adjusted the binoculars. With any luck, he'd be arriving from Hakozaki in just a few minutes.

"They're saying to keep driving. …I'm sorry, I don't know where the destination is, either."

Juri didn't hang up. It was a burner, so she didn't have to, but once this game ended, it needed to be disposed of immediately.

A silver-gray Mercedes entered my visual field. It was driving in the slow lane. I was sure it was the right car. I couldn't actually see the driver's face, but my intuition was telling me that it was

Katsuragi.

After counting in my head, I opened my mouth. "Tell him to get off at Mukojima after he passes Komagata. You know the rest of the instructions."

Confirming Juri's silent nod out of the corner of my eye, I took out my own phone. I made a call to a number that I'd recorded in the phone's memory.

"Yes, this is the Nissei Automobile Mukojima store," a young woman's voice answered.

"Excuse me, this is Tadokoro of the Nissei Automobile board of directors office. Is the manager present?"

As expected, the words "board of directors office" made her gasp.

"Ah, yes, please wait a moment."

Next to me, Juri gave her father instructions. "Papa, get off at Mukojima. ...Anyway, get off."

From my phone, I got a response: "Hello, this is the shop manager Nakamura."

"This is Tadokoro from the board of directors office. Excuse me for contacting you out of the blue. Actually, I have an urgent request to make."

"What would that be?" Nakamura's voice sounded strained.

"The executive vice president was driving in his own car in that area, but it broke down."

"The executive vice president's car..." Nakamura was speechless. It was probably a situation he'd never expected.

"We called the Japan Automobile Federation, so I believe it should be fine, but we have a certain issue."

"You got off at Mukojima? Then, go south down Bokutei Street. ...No, south. Double back."

With a sharp, low voice, Juri issued the instructions. Even as I listened to her, I continued with my own part.

"We would like you to quickly transport the luggage from his car to a certain location. When we checked the map, it seemed that your place was the closest, so we called."

"That, um, if that is the situation, I think I can do something, but, um, where should I go?"

"I'll call you later with a detailed address. For now, could you wait at the expressway entrance? For you, the Mukojima Interchange would be close."

"Yes, it is."

"All right, I'll contact you again, but um, who will be going?"

"Ah, I will, personally."

"In that case, Mr. Nakamura, may I please have your cellphone number?"

After getting his number, I told him mine. Of course, it wasn't my own number, but the one with the fictitious name Juri was currently using.

I hung up, and drinking beer, I listened to Juri's conversation.

"Yes, go on the expressway again from the Mukojima Interchange. ...I don't know why, either. I'm just saying what I'm being told to say."

I put the binoculars to my eyes. I couldn't see the Mercedes yet.

There still had to be a police tail on it. Exiting at Mukojima Interchange, then backtracking to get on the expressway again—if they tailed such an unnatural route, the police presence might be revealed to the culprit, but in a situation where there was no transmitter or bug, all they could do was to keep at it. While they were concerned for the hostage, I judged that the police would have the obstinacy to push forward.

Shaking them off was the final step.

I saw the Mercedes. I put out my hand to Juri. She gave the phone she had to me.

I put it to my ear. I took one deep breath. Then I opened my mouth.

"*Hello, Mister Katsuragi,*" I said in English.

A male voice all of a sudden, speaking in a different language to boot—there was no response.

I kept speaking. All of it was in English.

"*From here on I will speak in English. That should not be a problem, right? If the policemen tapping into this phone are proficient in English, then I'm an unlucky bastard, and I give up. Well, first, stop at the next parking area. It's the one that's coming up in three hundred meters. Stop at the very back of the merging lanes. If you understand, say yes.*"

"*Yes,*" Katsuragi answered using the English word.

"*Excellent.*"

With the binoculars, I looked at the Komagata parking area. The Mercedes put on its blinker and went in. However, no car followed after it. There wasn't even a car that entered prior to the Mercedes. It seemed that the tailing cars couldn't respond immediately. Just as planned.

"*Turn off the engine and leave the car without locking it. There's a rest stop area, so get in there.*"

I heard the sound of a door opening and closing. Then Katsuragi said in Japanese, "There's no point in any of this. There were never any police with me to begin with."

"*Don't chatter. Do as you're told.*"

"As long as Juri comes home, fine. I'm ready to pay the ransom."

"*I told you not to chatter. Instead, count. Count backwards from one thousand. In English.*"

"You don't have to do this, I won't contact the police."

"*Do as I say.*"

I heard Katsuragi sigh, then: "*One thousand. Nine hundred ninety-nine, nine hundred ninety-eight.*"

"*Go on.*"

Using the other phone, I called Nakamura.

"Hello, this is Tadokoro. Where are you right now?"

"Ah, um, I'm right next to Mukojima Interchange. I can get going at any time."

"What type of vehicle are you in?"

"A white minivan."

"Please get going immediately. The EVP's car is parked at Komagata PA. I don't think he's there, but his silver-gray Mercedes shouldn't be locked. Please take the cardboard box in there that was being transported."

"Where should I bring it?"

"There's a place called New Terminal Hotel near Kiyosubashi. There's a woman named Matsumoto waiting there so please give it to her."

"New Terminal Hotel at Kiyosubashi, then."

"I appreciate it. The EVP said he'd like to thank you personally at a later date."

"Thank me? No—"

"It's only natural. You saved us."

After hanging up, I winked at Juri. She handed over the phone, on which Katsutoshi Katsuragi was endlessly counting down in English. Then, she stood up and left the beer hall.

I ran the binoculars down the expressway. Eventually, I saw a white minivan heading in.

It entered the Komagata PA. Katsutoshi Katsuragi's countdown continued. I couldn't tell if he realized that he was about to be robbed of his money.

If the police were still on the ball by any chance, they would have to rush out now. However, as far as I could see, there was no sign of them.

The minivan left the parking area. Seeing that through, I stood up. I hung up the call with Katsutoshi Katsuragi.

I hailed a taxi and went back to my condo. I got into the MR-S and set out again.

I parked near New Terminal Hotel and approached slowly on foot.

It seemed Juri had seen me; the automatic door opened and she came out. Her arms were folded.

"The cargo?"

"Delivered." She grinned.

14

I checked to make sure there were no transmitters or bugs and transferred the bills into a different bag in my car. Throwing away the cardboard box, we went back to my condo. My pulse, as expected, had gone up a notch. I took many deep breaths to calm my heart. Juri was also silent in the car.

When we got back, she hugged me. "We did it. It was a huge success!" She was panting, and no wonder—she'd pulled off a major part.

I removed her arms from my neck. I looked into her eyes. They were bloodshot. "You did well. But let's hold off a bit on actually celebrating. The last finishing touches are still left."

"What are we doing?"

"For now, I'm going back to work. You can rest for a while."

"Can I count the money?"

"No, don't touch it for now. If you can't help it, put on gloves."

"Gloves?"

"I'll tell you the reason after I get home."

I kissed Juri on her lips and promptly took off.

I went back to the office, and with an innocent face, sat at my desk. No one seemed to care. It seemed the guys at Nissei Automobile hadn't returned yet.

I booted my computer and, after thinking for a while, started writing.

Mr. Katsutoshi Katsuragi,

We certainly received the cargo. We have not verified the contents yet. As soon as that work is done, we will return Juri Katsuragi. However, if we perceive any police action, that will not be possible. We will contact you again regarding our method of returning her to you.

I checked that there were no typos and, using an account with a fictitious identity, sent the email. I checked that it was sent safely and deleted the text from my computer. I would probably never use the account again.

A little past closing time, Kozuka and the others came back. Seeing my face, he approached my seat.

"Sorry about today."

"Not at all. Actually, how did the meeting go?"

"Well, we somehow decided on the direction. Starting tomorrow, we'll be busy with a lot of things."

"But don't you have to wait for Mr. Katsuragi's input? Because he left in the middle."

"No, he was able to return."

"Uh, he was?" I said in a falsetto.

"Yeah. He finished whatever he needed to do, so he was able to come back near the end of the meeting. So then, well, at that point we got their approval. It's good we didn't go there for nothing."

"I see…"

I couldn't believe it. That meant after handing over the ransom, Katsutoshi Katsuragi had gone straight back to work. How? Normally, having to talk to the police and dealing with the aftermath would have prevented him.

"Is something wrong?" Kozuka peered at my face curiously.

"No, nothing. I'm glad it went well," I said with a fake smile.

I left the office and headed home, but doubts were swirling in my head. I just couldn't find a satisfying explanation.

Katsutoshi Katsuragi's voice from that afternoon kept sounding in my ears.

There's no point in any of this. There were never any police with me to begin with.

As long as Juri comes home, fine. I'm ready to pay the ransom.

You don't have to do this, I won't contact the police.

Katsuragi had asserted multiple times that the police weren't involved. I hadn't believed those words and didn't believe them now. However, there were too many inconsistencies. When I had tried to use Hakozaki Junction to read my opponents' movements, it had been the same.

When I got home, Juri was sitting on the sofa watching TV. The banknotes were neatly piled on top of the center table. Three hundred million yen really was a spectacular sight.

"You didn't touch it with your bare hands, did you?"

"I put these on." Juri picked up rubber gloves. "But why can't I touch it with my bare hands?"

"Because we don't know what trick there might be. For instance, there might be stuff on it that changes color when you touch it with your hands. And then, that won't come off unless you use special solvents."

"Is there such a thing?" Juri looked at the notes with a spooked look.

"I've heard rumors. Other tricks are to use chemicals that change color after some time has passed. If we use this money without knowing about it, after some time, the party who took the money would find it suspicious and contact the police."

"There's a lot, isn't there."

"So it's best not to touch it for two or three days. If we wait just that long and nothing strange happens, then we can assume it's okay."

"You're really amazing," Juri said.

She actually sounded impressed, rather than teasing, so, feeling surprised, I looked at her face. "Why, that's sudden."

"You know everything and you're always two steps ahead. Even picking up the ransom money went that well. We have three hundred million yen in our hands almost without doing anything, using just cellphones."

"You don't need to flatter me to keep me from lowering your cut," I said laughing. "Two hundred seventy million yen. Suddenly you're rich."

"Are you sure I can take that much?"

"Compared to what you'd actually inherit, it's probably a paltry sum. I'm fine with thirty million yen. It's a good earning on top of playing a fun game."

"And you got Katsutoshi Katsuragi by his nose, too?"

"That's right." Even as I laughed, apprehension wafted through my heart. Was that right? Had I really won against Katsutoshi Katsuragi?

"Is something wrong?" Juri asked. She seemed to have noticed the change in my expression.

"I remembered that the game still isn't over. There's one last important part left." I put up my index finger. "Returning the hostage. We have to set you up as the pitiful victim. She was not only confined by heartless kidnappers but also coerced into helping extort the ransom. We need to get you back to the papa you love so dearly."

"I'll have to stay an actress for just a while longer, then." Juri puffed out her chest.

"This next act will be tough. I won't be by your side. No matter what happens, you'll have to get through it yourself. This act won't be for just a short time, either. Your whole life, you'll have to play the part of a kidnapping victim." I sat next to her, put my arm around her back, and pulled her towards me. "Are you ready for it?"

Juri blinked twice and stared at me. "Who do you think I am? I'm Katsutoshi Katsuragi's daughter."

"Right, of course," I nodded.

Returning Juri home wasn't hard. After putting her to sleep in a secluded place, I'd simply contact her father. Of course, I didn't really have to put her to sleep. If she just pretended, that would be enough.

The issue was after that. A rigorous performance would be required of her.

"First the police will ask you about the conditions under which you were abducted." I looked at her. "We went over those circumstances. Do you remember them? They'll ask why you snuck out of the house so late at night. Well, how will you respond?"

"That night…" As though she were remembering, she continued, "Chiharu and I had a little argument over cosmetic cream. I felt irritated, so I thought of going to this bar where I'm a regular. I snuck away because I didn't want my parents to get on my case."

Good, she aced that. As expected.

"Please tell us in detail what happened when you were kidnapped," I said, shoving an imaginary mic in her face.

"Just a little while after I left home, a car stopped next to me. When I wondered why and looked over, someone grabbed me from behind. I tried to scream, but something like a handkerchief had been placed over my mouth. I don't really remember what happened next." After thinking and speaking up to that point, she made a face as though to say, *How's that?*

"What's next is key, though. When you came to, you were at the culprits' hideout. They'll probably ask you what kind of place it was. How will you respond then?"

This bit was worth thinking out carefully. If it seemed unnatural, the police would start to have doubts. Those guys were at least aware that a kidnapping might have been staged. If we did the production on the fly, some contradiction might emerge.

"A blindfold," I said.

"What?"

"When you came to, you were blindfolded and couldn't see anything. That's how you'll answer. What's more, your hands are tied behind your back. In that state, you've been laid atop something like a bed."

"And my feet?"

"Aren't tied."

"Why not?"

"Because there's no need. Most people won't be able to move around at all if they can't see anything or use their hands. Tying your legs would be a bother to the kidnappers. Because they'd have to undo it and retie it every time you have to go to the bathroom."

Juri nodded. "Got it."

"When you tried to move, you heard a woman's voice—that's how you'll respond. The woman said, 'Don't get up from the bed. If you're obedient, we won't do anything to you.'"

"She's cool."

"That's right, she's a cool woman. When you think of a cool woman, whom do you visualize?"

Juri tilted her head a bit. "Makiko Esumi," she said. A little different from mine, but that was all right.

"Well, let's go with that. The police will ask you: Were there any special characteristics to her voice? How old do you think she is? Did she have an accent? At that time, you think of Makiko Esumi. You answer the police's questions like it was her voice you heard."

"What do I do if they ask if it's a voice I've heard before? Could I answer it's Makiko Esumi's voice?" Juri smiled impishly.

"Be my guest. The police would never knock on Esumi's door even if you did. Well, they can go bother her if they want."

"So the cool woman's task is to watch me."

"She's your jailer and caterer. Even though you didn't have an appetite, that woman had you eat, and you couldn't resist. You were eating with a blindfold on, so nothing really hot. Nothing that would be hard to eat. It was probably sandwiches. We'll say she untied your hands at least then. However, at those times, she tied up your legs instead. Yeah, let's go with that."

"When I eat, my hands are free, my legs are tied together..." It seemed Juri was picturing it in her head.

"Makiko Esumi had one more task. She was your conversation partner. We'll say she chose topics unrelated to the case and chatted with you. About actors, fashion, sports, that kind of thing."

"Boyfriends?"

"That's—" I shook my head. "We'll say she became less talkative whenever that topic came up. The woman wasn't acting alone, so the police will probably think that the principal offender was her boyfriend or husband. In which case, they'll want to know anything she said regarding love. That would be a hassle. A massive creative burden on you."

"I see." Juri seemed to be onboard. "Can I ask you something?"

"What is it?"

"When I went to the bathroom, did I have my blindfold on? How would I go about it when I couldn't see anything? Would Makiko Esumi have assisted me? I kind of don't like that."

I nodded with a strained smile. She had a point. It was a part we at least needed to pin something down for. "How about this? Whenever you said you wanted to go to the bathroom, the woman would take your hand and lead you to it. Your blindfold came off only after you got into the bathroom."

"So then the two of us would go in together?"

"It felt cramped, but what can I say? The kidnappers didn't want to give you any extra information. Once your blindfold was off, the woman would leave. After that, you had a little leisure time for yourself. You could pee, or whatever, to your heart's content."

"What a way to put it. You old perv."

"Naturally, you observe the bathroom interior. It was like this. The walls were concrete. There was just a small ventilation fan and no windows. The light was an incandescent lamp. They had amassed a reserve of toilet paper and even sanitary napkins. The toilet was Western style. It also came with a spray feature."

Juri clasped her hands as though in relief. It was probably hard for her to imagine taking care of her business without the spray feature. There would be more and more people like her with every passing year.

"The door was wooden. Originally it was made so that it locked from the inside. You know, the kind with a lateral bolt. However, the mechanism was taken out to keep you from holing up in there."

"I wonder if I can remember all that." Juri knit her brows, made fists with both hands, and held her head in between them. "I need a cheat sheet."

"The police will ask whether you heard anything when you were in the bathroom or when you were going to and from it."

"I can't go wrong with saying I heard nothing, right?"

I shook my head. "Once you're blindfolded, your hearing becomes fairly acute. If you tell them you heard nothing at all, they might get suspicious. It's better if you heard something."

Juri snapped her fingers. "Ships."

"Not bad." I nodded. This girl really was sharp.

"When we made the first call," Juri said, "we went to Yokosuka and had them hear the whistling. It was so they'd think the hideout was near a harbor, right? Then now too, wouldn't it be good to have the same thing?"

"You're right. But if you say you always heard it, that would be unnatural. The criminals would definitely have been wary of that.

You heard it once or twice, but it sounded distant. That's what you should tell them."

"Got it. Will that do on the sound front?"

"Just ship whistles and nothing else would be weird. The sound of cars passing by, let's add that too. Because places where you can't hear that are rare."

"Ships and cars." Juri had on her game face.

"All right, the cool woman isn't the only person you met. We need at least one more person to come on stage. That'll be the man."

"I know. The principal perpetrator who took the ransom."

"Principal perpetrator? That's quite a tongue twister. But he's exactly that. You've been forced to work with that perpetrator at least three times. Once was the time you initially called. The police will probably ask you to talk about that in detail."

"This has become really tiring." Juri made a dejected face and scratched her head.

"Those guys are desperate. The ransom money was just whisked away, okay? Forgive them for interrogating you."

"Sure. So, how should I explain it?"

"You say that you were told to call home. At that time, you heard the voice of the lead perp. Like with the cool woman, the police will probably ask what kind of voice he had."

"Who should I make it this time? How about Masaharu Fukuyama?" Her eyes lit up. She must have been a fan.

"In my mind he's in his forties, though. Is there a person you can think of?"

Juri moved her pupils around before slapping her knee. "I think the homeroom teacher I had my senior year in high school was around that age. He doesn't have to be famous, right?"

"Works for me. Well, that covers the first call. The next part is a little difficult. It's the Hakozaki conversation. That time, there's no way you didn't leave the hideout, so the police will probably be persistent."

"I guess 'I don't know anything' wouldn't pass muster?"

"But you still had your blindfold on. Additionally, they put headphones on you. Loud music was playing from them. It was obviously an arrangement on the criminals' part to keep you from hearing extra sounds. They had you get in the car like that and took you somewhere. You don't need to know too much about the place. You couldn't see or hear, so who's to blame you? There, they finally took off your headphones, but the blindfold stayed on. Eventually, the man gave you detailed instructions. Like I did then. You did what the man told you and talked to Katsutoshi Katsuragi on a cellphone."

"That time, you wrote what I was supposed to say on a note, though. If I were blindfolded, that wouldn't work."

"You were parroting the lines. You repeated exactly what the man said to you."

In any case, the police would probably check on the hotel we had used. There was no place else where you could monitor Hakozaki Junction. Plus, you could get to the guest floors of that hotel from an underground parking lot via an express elevator. Even if you were leading a girl who was wearing a blindfold and headphones, you could get through without anyone wondering about her strange getup.

The police would probably go to inquire at the hotel, but the staff would never figure out who we were. We'd left nothing they could latch on to.

"And lastly, the time we got the ransom money."

"Once again, I had a blindfold and headphones on when I was put in the car."

"Right. However, this time, you tell them you stayed inside. You were forced to call on the cellphone like that."

"Without going anywhere?"

"You felt that the car was constantly moving. Sometimes it stopped, but not for long. The police will interpret that as the criminal group traveling along the expressway while giving instructions for seizing the ransom. They won't be able to tell from where the group was watching Komagata PA or the whole expressway."

At that point, I heaved a sigh.

"That's it for you aiding the culprits."

"But actually there was one more time. A key part—my role in receiving the ransom."

"You didn't go as yourself, did you?"

"I did as you told me. I put on the plainest clothes ever, and you saw how I could change my makeup."

I nodded, satisfied. "That's fine then. That wasn't you. The woman named Matsumoto that Nakamura from Nissei Auto's Mukojima branch handed the cargo to was simply someone else. Her hair was long, and she had sunglasses on."

"A woman like this," Juri put on a wig that was by her side, and dark sunglasses.

"Not even the slightest resemblance to Makiko Esumi," I said with plenty of sarcasm, taking the items away from her. "We've got to dispose of these too. And the burner. What else do we have to dispose of—"

"Probably our history." Juri looked into my eyes as she said that.

15

Two full days had passed since we'd obtained the ransom money. There was no change in the bills. I timidly tried touching them with my hand, but nothing strange happened. It seemed no trap had been set.

I put my thirty million yen into a grocery bag. "This is my cut. That makes the rest of it all yours."

Juri laid her eyes on the tabletop and breathed a small sigh. "It's pretty cumbersome. And it looks heavy."

"It means we had that big of a match."

I passed a department store paper bag to her. She started putting the bills into it. Two hundred seventy million yen. It really would be quite heavy.

"What should I do with this money?"

"You can do whatever you want with it. It's yours. But you shouldn't use it in a flashy way."

Juri shook her head. "That's not what I mean. I can't just carry this money home. Am I going to keep it in a coin locker or something? And then get it after things have cooled down?"

"Coin lockers are dangerous. If by chance they find the key, then you're done for. And we don't know how long it'll take for things to cool down. Once the storage time has passed, it'll be opened. Game over."

"Then what should I do?"

"Do you have a sanctuary somewhere? A convenient place where only you go and only you know of? If you have a place like that you can store it there for a while."

After thinking for some time, she grinned. "There's just one place. A good place."

"Where?" As soon as I asked her, the answer came to me, and I frowned. "You want to say this condo, but we can't do that. After getting you back safely, we won't ever get in touch again. We said so from the beginning, remember?"

"But there's no other good place."

It seemed she really had set her sights on my room. "Okay. Get ready to go out."

"Where are we going?"

"You'll know if you follow me." I stood up. "Don't forget the two hundred seventy million yen."

I left my room and headed to the parking lot. I looked at the clock. It was nine thirty at night.

"Hey, where are we going? You can tell me, can't you?"

"Yokosuka."

"Yokosuka…again?"

"You said that you had that friend who went to America, right? Was her name Yuki? We went to erase your message."

Ah, comprehension finally came over her face. "So we're going to hide it in Yuki's room."

"That's the safest, isn't it?"

The answering machine incident had been a headache, but now I was glad that room existed. I'd been worried about the hiding place for the money the entire time.

We got into the MR-S and, like we had that night, drove with the roof up. Juri was preciously hugging the money in the paper bag on her knees. It was her livelihood from here on out.

"Hey, I wonder if the police investigation has started," she said.

"Of course. It should have when we sent the kidnappers' fax."

"Do you think they've found a clue?"

"There's no way they would." I curled my lips. "If they did, it's a fake clue. The faint sound of ships in the background, and such."

There was no worry about them coming at us via the emails or cellphones. The sole witness was Nakamura from the Nissei Muko-jima branch, but if Juri was to be believed, the man wouldn't be able to furnish useful information to the police.

"But there is one clear clue," Juri said.

"What's that?"

"The culprit speaks English. With a British accent."

At that, I jerked the steering wheel. The body of the car swerved widely off the centerline. I immediately righted it.

"Are you good at English?" I asked, feigning calm.

"Not really. I honestly don't know much about accents. I just thought it kind of sounded British. Am I wrong?"

"Well, maybe." I felt sweat running down my leg.

She was right. I'd lived near London for a year. You could say that was when I'd become proficient in English. Some people could tell.

I changed expressways, and we arrived at Yokosuka. I saw the restaurant we had stopped at before. I remembered that someone had sprayed my MR-S.

"Could you wait there again?" Juri said.

"No, that place is bad luck, so let's not do that. I'll drive up close tonight."

"Close…"

"Next to Yuki's condo. Carrying a package that big is difficult, isn't it?"

"I'm fine. If you wait next to the condo, with this kind of car you'll stand out."

"I'm more scared of you standing out. You're just leaving the package in the room, right? If I'm only parked for a short time, no one will get suspicious. Tell me the way."

"Oh, uhh, turn right at that corner."

"Right, is it?" I turned on the blinker and entered the right lane.

However, from that point it was a disaster. Juri's navigation was unreliable. She made mistakes about which corners to turn on and we got lost. In the end it took over thirty minutes to get to the condo after wandering around. Juri's excuse was that she'd never gone there by car.

"Even so, that was terrible. Oh well. It's that condo?" I turned my eyes to the right side of the road. There was a white building that looked at least four stories high, but it seemed like there weren't many units. It was almost midnight, and about half the rooms still had lights on in the windows.

"Well, I'm going."

"Be careful."

From inside the car, I watched Juri's back as she carried the heavy-looking paper bag. Fortunately, there were few residences in the area. It was late and it seemed we didn't have to worry about people seeing us.

I gazed at the condo. I hadn't asked the room number, so I didn't know which floor Juri intended to go up to. In a four-story building, there might not be an elevator. Carrying that package up the stairs would probably be hard.

I stayed like that for about five minutes, then thought, *That's weird*. There wasn't a new light turning on in any window. Yuki's room would probably be dark, so Juri should have turned on the light immediately.

Maybe I just couldn't see it from this side?

About five more minutes later, Juri came out. She crossed the street at a jog and approached my car.

"Sorry for making you wait," she apologized, getting into the passenger seat. It seemed she was a little out of breath.

"Did you hide it okay?" I said, starting the car.

"Yeah, perfectly."

"Wouldn't Yuki's parents or someone go in?"

"That's okay. She said that would never happen. Even if someone did go in, I hid it where they wouldn't be able to find it easily."

"Is Yuki's room that big?"

"It isn't, but it's pretty disorganized with furniture everywhere."

"And the floor plan?"

"Huh?"

"The floor plan of Yuki's room. Is it a studio?"

"Ah, uhh, it is. What about it?"

"No, I was wondering what kind of rooms young people live in around here."

If it was a studio, then if the light were turned on, it would be visible from outside, I thought.

After we had driven for a while, Juri said, "Hey, do you want to try going there?"

"There?" I stepped on the brake.

"That place. You remember, right? We went there the last time we came."

"Ah…" Of course I hadn't forgotten it or anything. "Why there?"

"Because, tonight is the last night. I have to go home and we won't meet again."

I was silent. It was as she said. I was thinking about escorting her somewhere tonight and contacting Katsutoshi Katsuragi. With that the game would be over.

"So, I thought we might go to that place with those memories." She said it in a somewhat offhand tone. It might have been out of embarrassment.

I took my foot off the brake pedal. Yokosuka was a decoy location for us, so it was better not to hang around for too long. But I thought maybe a short while was okay. Just as she said, this was our last night together.

I stopped the car on the hill at the tip of Miura Peninsula half an hour later. Like that other night, I let down the hood completely and took in the grassy scent. Next to me, Juri was taking a deep breath too.

Unfortunately, it seemed that there were clouds spread across the sky. Tonight we couldn't see the stars.

"It was a short time, but it was so much fun," Juri said looking at my face.

"It was a thrilling game."

"I think every day after tomorrow will feel really boring."

"It won't be. I'll keep saying it, but you still have a job left to do."

"That's nothing. Compared to what I've been up to."

"That's promising." I laughed.

"Mr. Sakuma." Her eyes gleamed with sincerity. "Thanks for everything."

"That's hardly necessary. I got fun out of this, too. It's been a pleasure playing a do-or-die match for the first time in a while."

"Plus you won the match?"

"Yeah."

We faced each other and smiled.

"But really, thank you," Juri said. "Because of you, I can keep on living."

"That's a little extreme."

"But it's the truth... I guess I shouldn't expect you to understand." She tilted her head.

Our gazes met and, just like that, we kissed. Her lips were soft and slightly moist. I felt myself stiffening, but didn't think of trying to undress her. It was always important to know when to quit. I had to cut off our relationship here. I shouldn't be so wistful.

But still, just once more, for the last time, I held Juri's body tightly. It seemed she'd lost some weight these past few days. "Thank you," she whispered again as our bodies parted.

We got off the Coastal Way at Oiminami and headed to Shinagawa station. But instead of stopping there, I parked when a large hotel came into view on my left.

"Okay, one last review," I said.

"Again? You're so damn persistent." Juri strained a laugh.

"Persistence is our lifeline. Please don't complain—can we just do this?"

"When I woke up..." Her eyes grew distant. "I was lying inside a car. I think it was probably a Mercedes. My hands and feet weren't tied up, and no one else was there. So I got out of the car. I was dizzy, but thinking that it was my last chance, I started running for my life. Because of that, I didn't have the time to read the car's plate. It seemed like I was in a parking lot. Actually, it was a hotel's basement parking lot. I used an elevator to go to the lobby, but it was the middle of the night, so no one was there. I left through the front entrance and headed toward the taxi pickup. I didn't think about whether I had money or not. I thought that as long as I got home, it would be okay."

She grinned and looked at me. "Was there anything I got wrong?"

"No, that was perfect." I gave her an okay sign. "You have the letter?"

"Yeah, I'm all set."

I'd handed her a letter. The text, which I'd composed on my computer, read as follows:

To Mr. Katsutoshi Katsuragi,

   We did indeed receive the ransom. As promised, we will return Juri Katsuragi.

The reason we did not act violently toward her will likely be made clear through her own mouth. We acknowledge that this transaction proceeded in a highly businesslike manner.

It was a fun game. We consider it nothing less than complete. After this, there will be no contact from us. We promise never to choose you as a player again.

From,

The Kidnappers

"Then it's finally time," I said.

"Yeah. Take care."

"You too. Good luck."

We shook hands. Her gaze lingering on our hands, Juri got out of the car. *Thank you, goodbye*—with those words, she closed the door. I moved the car out.

The city at night spread before me.

16

On Saturday I went on a date for the first time in a while. She was a twenty-four-year-old event companion. We feasted on Italian fare and had several cocktails at the hotel bar, but it didn't develop into us staying over at the hotel. Even if we'd wanted to, there probably wouldn't have been any open rooms. I'd always put in a reservation when I was confident I'd score, but I hadn't made those preparations that night. It wasn't because I wasn't confident. For some reason it just felt like a pain.

Honestly, it wasn't that I harbored any special feelings for the woman. Anyone could have been my date.

I was in a mood, so even eating wasn't much fun, and I couldn't get excited about talking. She was probably wondering until the end why I'd called her.

I couldn't get Juri out of my head. What had happened since then? Oddly enough, there hadn't been any reports at all about the case. By all rights, the press should've been having a party. The great Nissei Automobile's executive vice president's daughter had been kidnapped, and furthermore, the ransom had been stolen. It was hard to think that there was a gag order. The hostage had returned safe and sound, so the police, themselves, could transition to a public investigation. Shouldn't they be making active use of the press?

When I parted from the event companion and got back to my room, I booted my computer and connected to the internet. I tried accessing the CPT Owners Club. Since successfully seizing the ransom, I hadn't revisited it once.

I opened the bulletin board page. There was an endless stream of unrelated comments. Unrelated to Juri—actually, those were the legitimate ones.

My hand froze on my mouse. It was because I saw this post:

> Please (Julie)
> I wonder what's happened to my dear car. They haven't gotten in touch even though I paid the money and I wonder what's happening.
> The car's owner, if you see this post, please contact me. Please.

What did it mean?

When I looked at the date, it was from the night before. The text was no doubt begging that Juri be returned without delay. However, she should have safely returned to the Katsuragis.

Was it a trap?

That was possible—pretending that Juri hadn't come home and hoping the culprits would resume contact.

But, I thought. Even if Juri hadn't gotten home, that wasn't the kidnappers' problem. Wasn't it incredibly naïve to expect them to reply? In fact, I felt no desire to take any sort of action.

But what if Juri hadn't gotten home?

I thought that was the more likely possibility. I had dropped her off by a hotel in Shinagawa, but she might not have gotten in a taxi there. No, even if she had, there was no knowing if she'd headed on home. She hated the Katsuragis. She'd come into a lot of money and might have decided to just vanish.

If that were the case, it was a catastrophe. The psychology of a victim who'd been kidnapped and who'd finally gotten away from

186

the culprits should have been to return to safety. Even if it wasn't a very comfortable home, the Katsuragi residence had to be Juri's sole refuge.

If Juri stayed missing, that would be fine. The truth would never come to light. But wouldn't that be hard? Could a girl who was barely twenty keep her identity hidden? Even if she had a lot of money, without a certificate of residence or family register, how did she intend to live?

At this rate, the police would have to dive into an open investigation. Pictures of Juri's face would likely appear all over Japan. TV stations wouldn't leave the case alone. No matter how much Juri tried to conceal herself, she'd still have to go outside. She'd have to come into contact with people. Someone would definitely recognize her.

What performance did she intend to act out once she was in the custody of the police? Did she mean to start using, only then, the lines I'd fed her? It would be meaningless. The police would eventually suspect the kidnapping was a ruse. I didn't think Juri could withstand their relentless interrogation. It was just a matter of time before she gave me up.

Unable to sit still, I took my coat in hand and ran out of the room. I was completely sober.

I got into the MR-S and headed towards Yokosuka yet again. If Juri were in hiding, I didn't think it'd be anywhere other than that condo. The money was also hidden there.

Speeding down the expressway, I organized my next steps in my mind. Finding Juri came first. What would I do once I found her? At any rate, I'd have to make her go home, even if I needed to spank her. I could only spin the extended confinement as an outcome of the culprits' extreme cautiousness.

Even so, if Juri had already met with someone, it was over. I didn't think she could be that stupid, but what would I do in that case? My brain was in full gear, but I couldn't think of a genius plan. I could only pray that she hadn't seen anyone.

I arrived at Yuki's condo. I parked my car a little ways away and walked from there. Wandering around a place like this was dangerous, but leaving Juri alone was riskier. Whatever happened, I had to take her home.

Making sure that no one saw me, I approached the building. It was the middle of the night, so the superintendent probably wasn't there. But the problem was that I didn't know the room number. What I did know was the given name or nickname Yuki.

The glass door of the entrance had been left open. It didn't seem to be auto-locking. Just as I thought, the super wasn't there. The mailboxes were lined up to the right. There were nametags on some but not all of them. Even when there was one, when it was just the surname it served me no use.

Mindful of my surroundings, I plunged my hand into a mail slot on one end. Though I groped around with my fingers, I couldn't feel anything. It was Saturday night. Probably all the mail had been picked up.

I moved to the next mailbox. This time I felt something. When I grabbed it with my fingertips and brought it out, it was a postcard. I looked at the addressee. It was for Kaoru Yamamoto. That couldn't be Yuki.

Next I put my hand into the mailbox beside that. I became anxious. Would I ever get anywhere this way? But it was all I could do.

My fingertips touched something. I carefully pulled it out. This time it was an envelope.

Tetsuya Matsumoto—

I returned it thinking that wasn't it, either. At that moment, something suddenly came to me.

It's better if you don't come. Because it's a women-only condo—
Juri had definitely said that.

17

Ten days had passed since we had successfully obtained the ransom. My regular life had returned to what it was before the game. Wake up, light exercise, breakfast, go out the door. At the company I did boring work and I'd stop by the gym on the way home. I intended to invite someone out on a date over the weekend. This time, I planned on enjoying myself up to sex. I'd probably need to make a reservation at some hotel.

The days were tranquil; my mind was anything but. I was worried about Juri. Why didn't they report on it at all? I didn't think the police needed to censor the press. I was worried about the post on the CPT Owners Club, too. According to the last message, it seemed like Juri hadn't gotten home at all. What had happened after that? Since then, there hadn't been a new post.

If Juri were home, that would be okay. Katsutoshi Katsuragi might have pulled some strings to keep the press quiet. Because if a girl that age were kidnapped, everyone would expect something to have happened to her.

But I had the feeling I shouldn't be too optimistic.

One cause of my anxiety was the Yokosuka condo. According to Juri, her friend Yuki was renting in a women-only condo, but when I looked into it, there were a good number of men living there. And part of the building was even company-owned housing for a steel manufacturer. Juri had said Yuki's room was a studio, but when I asked the super about it at a later date, he said there were no such units at all.

Why had Juri told such a lie?

I retraced my memory. What she'd said about the condo being for women only had gone something like this:

But it's better if you don't come. Because it's a women-only condo. You could just chill at Yokosuka harbor and gaze at the passing ships.

Basically, she had just not wanted me to go with her and made up that lie on the spot. Why had she not wanted me to come?

I recalled what had happened the time we had gone to Yokosuka again on the last day. On that occasion, I'd tried to go to the condo with her. Her navigation had suddenly become erratic. On the way there we'd actually gotten lost. Why had that happened?

My theory was that she'd been searching for a random condo. She hadn't wanted me to go to Yuki's condo no matter what, so she'd found one similar to Yuki's and tricked me. If so, that condo not being women-only and not having studios made sense. It did, but then new doubts arose. Why had she gone so far to keep me from going to Yuki's condo? And where had she hidden the two hundred seventy million yen she'd been carrying?

Was there some secret about Yuki's condo that she didn't want to share with me? But what sort of secret necessitated not even allowing me to go to the building?

At that point, I tried questioning the fundamentals of the situation. Did Yuki's condo actually exist? No, to begin with, was this friend, Yuki, real?

Juri had given that name when the game had only just started. She had confessed to calling her friend and leaving a message on the answering machine. When I proposed canceling the whole plan, Juri had said we could just go to the room and erase the message. So we'd gone all the way to Yokosuka.

If Yuki was an imaginary person, that meant the answering

machine story was also a lie. Why tell that particular lie?

There was just one thing I could think of. She simply wanted to take me to Yokosuka. What would have been the point, though? Going there had served the tactical use of misdirecting the police as to the location of the culprits' hideout. But that was my idea and not Juri's suggestion. To grasp at straws, the only suggestion she did make was to go to a hill where you could see the stars. What was that about? What had that done?

No matter how I thought about it, the Yuki part didn't seem like a made-up story. Then why had Juri made up a lie about the condo? At that point my thoughts went in circles. I felt like I was wandering in a labyrinth far away from the goal.

There was one more cause for my anxiety. It was Katsutoshi Katsuragi.

According to the people involved in the new Nissei Automobile car release, Katsuragi hadn't attended meetings at all since last weekend. There were rumors that he hadn't been coming to work either. Why had that man, who hadn't let his style suffer even as I inflicted my kidnapping game on him, started taking time off from work now that it was over?

The faces of the father and daughter pair, Katsutoshi and Juri Katsuragi, alternately drifted through my mind. I didn't know what the two of them were thinking. I couldn't begin to guess where they were now and what they were up to. That fact harried me to no end.

"Excuse me, could you please lift your left hand a little more? Ah, that's right. That's perfect." The bearded cameraman clicked the shutter in succession.

The person being photographed was a popular pro golfer who had recently become active outside of Japan as well. He held a putter and made a pose as though he'd just gotten the ball in the hole. He seemed accustomed to being photographed, and there was little awkwardness in his expression. I took comfort in knowing that the shoot probably wouldn't take long.

It was for a magazine promo for a wristwatch made by a German company. Because they wanted to highlight its impact- and vibration-resistance, we had a golfer promote it. We were showing how, even with his powerful swing, the watch was invulnerable.

After the shoot was the interview. Beforehand, we had the pro-golfer put on the watch and hit some balls. We would ask about how that felt. Of course, it wasn't me who would ask; the assigned writer would also conduct the interview. While that happened in a tearoom in the studio, I attended to the wristwatch-only shoot. A junior coworker of mine named Yamamoto would be there for the interview.

It seemed around the time our shoot was done, the interview had ended. After seeing the pro golfer off to the entrance, I had a meeting with the writer about the content. He was a young man with long hair. After we had spoken for a bit, I feared that he might be missing the point, so I instructed him in detail about what aspects to emphasize. The writer seemed dissatisfied, but an article meant to showcase his own literary sensibilities was worthless.

"Mr. Sakuma, you're as harsh as ever. That writer was hoping to delve into a pro golfer's true face and was focusing his questions on that," Yamamoto divulged bemusedly in the car on the way back to the office. He was driving.

"We're not letting a guy like him tamper with our precious ad. I bet he wants to make it as a nonfiction writer one day, but if he can't grasp the point of an assignment, no wonder he hasn't gotten there yet."

"Haha, I guess you could say that." Yamamoto laughed like it was the funniest thing, then lowered his voice a little and added, "By the way, Mr. Sakuma, did you hear about Mr. Katsuragi?"

"Mr. Katsuragi? The executive vice president?" I asked with a start.

"Yes, of course. It seems that something happened to his daughter."

Now my heart skipped a beat. "Like what?"

"I don't really know, but it seems she's gone missing."

I faced Yamamoto. If he had been looking at me, he might have noticed that I'd gone pale. Luckily, his eyes were on the street.

"Missing?" My voice sounded an octave too high.

"I don't know the details. I only heard about it from someone else, and he told me it was just a rumor at Nissei Automobile. But it seems like a concrete story, and they're saying that's why Mr. Katsuragi hasn't been showing up to work lately. He did or didn't put in a missing person report, and so on."

"Why would that become a rumor? Did Mr. Katsuragi tell someone?"

"He must have. Assuming the rumors are true."

"When did you hear about this?"

"This morning. Before setting out for this job. I wanted to see if you'd heard about it but didn't get the chance. The way you're acting now, I suppose you hadn't."

"I didn't know at all."

"I see. It's just a rumor though." Yamamoto continued to drive unaware of the importance of what had come out of his mouth.

I was lucky he hadn't asked me before the shoot. If he'd told me, I wouldn't have been in any state to work and wouldn't have possessed the judgment to tell off that incompetent writer.

Yamamoto was talking about something else. Contributing to the conversation as necessary, I thought about Juri. She was missing? So she really hadn't gone home. Then where was she?

The scene of our parting near Shinagawa station revived in my mind. Where had she gone from there? Had she been snatched away by someone? Impossible. Getting abducted right after a staged kidnapping was a story too tall even for TV dramas.

She had to have disappeared of her own volition. Where to? At that point, the words "Yuki's condo" grabbed me again.

What if Juri had planned this scenario from the start?

She had gotten on board with my kidnapping game. However, she hadn't been interested in becoming my puppet. She'd meant to disappear somewhere instead of going home once she'd gotten the money. But until she could find a permanent destination, she needed a place to hide away. She chose her friend's condo. That was why its location had to be concealed from me. She thought that if I knew, I would come looking for her when I found out that she hadn't gone home. Indeed, I went to Yokosuka.

With this theory, I at least had an explanation. But there was one point that still didn't make sense.

If the theory was correct, she didn't have to tell me about Yuki's condo at all. Or was the part that she'd left a message on the answering machine true? No, even then, she wouldn't have had to rush there. She could erase it at her leisure if she meant to use it as a hiding place later.

I must have been grunting noncommittally because Yamamoto stopped talking.

When I got back to the office and arrived at our floor, I was taken aback. No one was there.

"Huh, what happened?" Yamamoto said, also sounding confused.

But it was just our misunderstanding that the place had been vacated; everyone had gathered in one corner. There was a TV set there, but the screen wasn't even visible to me thanks to the layers of people.

"Did something happen?" Yamamoto called out to one of them.

"Yeah, it's intense. That rumor was actually true."

"That rumor?"

"About Mr. Katsuragi's daughter. They say she's gone missing. And it's been over ten days."

"What?!"

Yamamoto pushed his way through. I followed him. Finally, I could see the TV screen. But there was just an announcer's face informing us about a different case. It seemed the segment on Juri Katsuragi had ended.

The congregation around the TV started returning to their seats, musing about the whole thing.

"Work must be the last thing on Mr. Katsuragi's mind now."

"I thought it was weird for that man not to come to meetings."

"Won't Nissei's stock go down again?"

"I wonder, did she just run away?"

"Let's hope so. She hasn't been murdered or anything, has she?"

The last, alarming speculation came from Sugimoto. I grabbed his shoulder.

"Hey, tell me the details. What's up with Mr. Katsuragi's daughter?"

Sugimoto looked at me with some surprise. "It seems she's been missing since several days ago, and the police have begun investigating."

"Investigating? What kind of investigation is this?"

"I don't know. It's probably showing on other channels." Sugimoto went back to his seat like he couldn't be bothered.

Ah, Yamamoto let out behind me. It seemed he'd been changing the channel busily, and a different announcer from before was displayed. *Nissei Auto EVP's daughter missing,* the title said.

The female announcer reported pretty much what Sugimoto had told me. *We have learned that Mr. Katsutoshi Katsuragi's elder daughter, Juri, has gone missing. The Metropolitan Police Department and the Ota Police Station believe that she has been involved in a case and have launched an investigation—*

Involved in a case?

What did it mean? Why didn't they just say that it was a kidnapping? No, more importantly, Juri was missing. What in the world had happened to her?

Yet it was what followed the next moment that truly stunned me. A woman's face appeared on screen.

It seemed to be a candid photo. *Juri Katsuragi*, the caption said.

The female announcer's report continued. However, her voice didn't reach my ears. If no one were next to me, I might have screamed at the TV screen. Holding back that urge took a great deal of effort.

The face of Juri Katsuragi on the TV screen didn't belong to the Juri I knew. It was the face of a completely different person whom I'd never met.

18

I needed a drink, but I went straight home. If I got drunk carelessly, I might run my mouth about something I shouldn't. I didn't have the confidence tonight to keep my emotions under check.

Once I was home, I took out a bottle of bourbon and started drinking it straight. My heart was still thumping. Or maybe this was what they called a premonition. If that was what it was, it wouldn't help no matter how much I drank.

The TV screen was burned into my mind and refused to go away. The face of Juri Katsuragi that had been displayed.

Who *was* that? Why was a different person's face being presented to the public as hers?

But I kept seeing the same face on other news programs. If they had broadcast another person's by mistake, they'd have corrected it by now.

In other words, that was Juri Katsuragi.

Then the person I spent several days with wasn't Juri? Who was it, then? Why had she presented herself as Juri?

Was there any way I might ascertain if she had been the real Juri? Eventually I thought of one. Her voice.

In order to spy on the police's behavior, we had used Hakozaki Junction. At that time, I had used Juri to manipulate Katsuragi. For grabbing the ransom money, too. Juri had spoken with Katsuragi. He hadn't seemed to doubt that it was her. Even if the two women had similar voices, I didn't think that a father would mistake his own daughter's. Even if he had been at his wits' end—and as far as I could tell, Katsutoshi Katsuragi hadn't lost sight of himself. Down to just before his ransom money was taken, he'd responded to my instructions collectedly.

Then was the photo broadcast on TV wrong? Had Katsutoshi Katsuragi intentionally provided a different person's pic? Why would he ever do such a thing?

No, that was definitely unthinkable. I wasn't the only one tuning in. Juri's acquaintances were, too. If the person in the photo were different, someone would call the station right away.

Juri. As in the first characters from "arbor" and "science."

I recalled how she'd told me her name at the beginning. She'd definitely said so. Was that a lie, too? Had the lies started so early?

Who could that have been?

No matter how much bourbon I gulped down, I still felt sober. My pulse quickened, while I grew more and more unsettled.

I recollected the hours and days I had spent with her. It was a short time, but a lot had happened. We had played an audacious game, a staged kidnapping, to completion. What did it mean that I didn't know my partner's true identity?

That wasn't the only thing I didn't know. It seemed that somehow the real Juri Katsuragi had vanished the same night I had met the fake Juri. Where had the real Juri gone? Was the fake Juri running away from home coincidental or inevitable?

My brain was a disorganized mess. I couldn't come up with a single logical answer.

I lost track of how much alcohol I'd imbibed. When I came to, I was lying on the sofa. I had left the light on, and the bottle of bourbon was on its side and empty. The sun was shining through from the other side of the curtain. I looked at the wall clock. It wasn't even ten minutes off from the usual hour I woke up. It seemed ingrained habits didn't break down even at a time like this.

I got up sluggishly. My head hurt horribly. My throat was completely parched. I went to the kitchen and pulled out Evian water and drank it straight out of the bottle. I felt dizzy and leaned on the refrigerator.

My eyes rested on the large pot that sat on top of the microwave. I recalled Juri had used it to make stew. The various things she'd talked about passed through my head. How much of it was true, which parts were lies? Or had it all been lies? As I was now, I couldn't judge.

I went back to the sofa and turned on the TV. In the early morning, every station repeatedly broadcast the same news. As I watched absentmindedly, the case in question came up, too. *Nissei Auto EVP's daughter missing*—now there was a question mark appended to the words. And beneath them: *Running away from home?*

And again, the photo of a girl I had never met before popped up. *The missing Juri Katsuragi*, it was captioned. There wasn't anything new in the story. It seemed they hadn't spoken to the Katsuragis. They must have been wary of approaching the family behind a leading corporate sponsor. There were signs the media were frustrated about not being able to obtain detailed information.

Perhaps the press hadn't been told that it was a kidnapping. I vaguely saw why. The police wanted their blunder of losing the ransom to be kept under wraps. They probably thought that bit could wait until the culprits' arrest. But to conduct an open investigation, they needed the mass media. Thus they had simply made it public that she was missing.

Starting with TV, the issue was how the press would cover it, I thought. They wouldn't accept just being used. They probably had a hunch that this wasn't exactly a missing person case. First, they would try to find out more about the Katsuragi household. It was a matter of time before Katsutoshi Katsuragi's womanizing ways came to light. Once they learned that Juri wasn't his current wife's daughter, the daytime shows would have a field day. The stations would compete at the art of dishing out gossip without angering a leading corporate sponsor.

No—

Was that story true in the first place? The person who'd shared it with me was herself a fake. Yet, for a quick lie, it was well crafted. Irregular blood ties, a complex human tapestry—

It was then that a certain hypothesis came to me.

19

That afternoon, I went to Akasaka, to a café facing out toward Soto-bori Street. About ten minutes past two, I saw Daisuke Yuguchi's fat figure on the other side of the glass door. Yuguchi spotted me right away, waved his hand, and entered.

"Sorry for making you wait."

"No, thanks for agreeing to see me on such short notice."

Yuguchi worked at a TV station right nearby. He had graduated after me from the same college, but we had also worked together just once.

He ordered coffee, so I ordered a refill of mine.

After some small talk, I started on the issue at hand. "So, about the favor I asked for on the phone, did you find out anything?"

As soon as I said that, Yuguchi frowned. "It looks like my station is hard at it. But the Katsuragis and the police both have their guards up, and we haven't dug up anything concrete."

"But it's not like all your info gets broadcast. Aren't there some bits you just haven't reported yet?"

If you know anything about the Juri Katsuragi case, please tell me, I had asked of him. Yuguchi hadn't suspected me at all when I said I needed to know all I could in advance about whatever happened to the family of the EVP of our biggest client, Nissei Auto.

"The guys at the top of the news division might have heard something, but nothing's come down to the lower ranks. Umm, you know the basics of the situation, right, Mr. Sakuma?" Yuguchi said as he pulled out a note.

"I know the gist of it. But just in case, do tell me what's happened so far."

"That's fine. Umm, first, Juri went missing when…"

Yuguchi started reading his note out loud. There was nothing new in it, but I continued to feign interest. "How about a kidnapping? Could it be one?"

"It's hard to say, but I doubt it," Yuguchi replied rather confidently.

"Meaning?"

"This is just between me and you." After looking around, he leaned towards me. "According to the press club guys, the Metropolitan Police Department's abductions unit hasn't mobilized. If it were a kidnapping, the investigation would have started when Juri was abducted about ten days ago, so there's no way the press club guys wouldn't have caught on. The MPD is definitely acting now, but it doesn't seem like there are detectives at the Katsuragi residence keeping watch, for instance."

"The MPD's abductions unit didn't act when she went missing? Are you sure?"

"Yes, that's what's being said."

It felt like something was toppling over in my head. The MPD hadn't acted? There was no way. This was a child of the Katsuragi family who had been kidnapped, so in fact it wasn't inconceivable for them to have mobilized their investigative capacities on a massive scale. That couldn't have avoided the notice of reporters covering the MPD.

If what Yuguchi was saying was true, there was only one possibility I could think of. Just as Katsutoshi Katsuragi had insisted, he hadn't contacted the police. He'd done so only after paying the ransom. Yet Juri hadn't come home, and he hadn't been able to endure it any longer. It really seemed that way.

Why hadn't he contacted the police? Was it because he thought that Juri would be in danger if he did and the kidnappers found out?

"The whole thing is a mystery," Yuguchi continued. "According to our guys, Mr. Katsuragi reported it to the police only a few days ago. Everyone's wondering why he didn't do so immediately after she went missing."

"And Mr. Katsuragi hasn't given an explanation."

Yuguchi thrust his bottom lip forward and shook his head. "No explanations, and he's turned down all requests for interviews. The official statement is that there's no need to talk about anything beyond what's been reported."

I growled and crossed my arms. Why hadn't Katsutoshi Katsuragi sought any help from the police for the kidnapping? Did he believe he could just pay the ransom and get his daughter back? Did he decide that telling the police could wait until it was over?

I shook my head in my mind. There was no way. I didn't think Katsutoshi Katsuragi, of all people, would succumb to threats. He was confident when it came to games. In a battle of wits with the culprit, he wouldn't have thrown in the towel from the outset.

There was something here. And that thing had everything to do with Juri being a fake.

"Did you get any info on the Katsuragi family?"

"Oh, that wasn't very difficult. They'd already looked into it." Yuguchi pulled out a new note and placed it in front of me.

It had a list of names: Katsutoshi Katsuragi, wife Fumiko, elder daughter Juri, younger daughter Chiharu.

"He has another daughter?" I asked innocuously, glancing at the note.

"It seems that way. She attends a private high school. She's a senior, I heard."

"Senior... I wonder which school."

"It was definitely—" Yuguchi gave the school's name. It was a high school affiliated with a famous women's college.

Asking just about Chiharu Katsuragi would have been strange, so I inquired about Juri and the wife as well. But Yuguchi didn't have many details. I knew more than he did.

"The wife and younger sister must be so worried that Juri has gone missing," I said.

"Apparently, the younger sister was quite shocked. She's been bedridden since her sister went missing."

"Bedridden? Chiharu?"

"Yes. Some of the press barged in on Chiharu's high school to get her to talk about her family. But Chiharu had taken a sick day. She's been taking time off for ten days now, so she must actually be sick rather than avoiding the press."

I tried my best to keep a straight face, with Yuguchi there. I felt incredibly thirsty, so I finished my glass of water.

"Can I have this?" I reached my hand toward the note.

"Go ahead. But it must be really difficult for all of you, Mr. Sakuma. For a case like this to occur right before the Nissei Automobile new car campaign."

"It does feel like a bad break." I didn't tell him I'd been taken off the project. I didn't have any reason to.

I thanked him for doing this when he was busy, took the receipt, and stood up.

Exiting the café and hailing a cab, I gave my company's address. As the car went out, I pulled out the note Yuguchi had just given me. Gazing at it, I changed my mind.

"Excuse me, driver, I have a change of destination. Please go to Meguro."

"Meguro? Where in Meguro?"

I gave the name of a particular women's high school. It seemed the driver knew it.

Naturally, it was the one Chiharu Katsuragi attended.

When the school was about a hundred feet away, I got out of the taxi. It seemed it was already past the final bell, and I saw gaggles of students heading home.

There was a small bookstore, so pretending to peruse a magazine, I kept an eye out for a high school girl I might talk to. The world saw this academy as a place for rich kids, but many had dyed hair and makeup done in the style of popular artists and didn't seem any different from other girls their age. The school must have loosened its regulations.

After the stream of students had trailed off a bit, a pair of girls came by. Both of them had brown hair. They had well-formed but somehow vulnerable features; if they went to an entertainment district, they would get hit on at least once an hour. They were no doubt confident about their looks. I made my decision and approached them.

"Excuse me," I spoke to them with a smile.

They both stopped walking and cast dubious looks at me.

"I'm not anyone to be worried about. It's just that I do this type of work."

The business card I brought out was for a rival station of Yuguchi's. Faced with high school girls, there was no better weapon than working for the popular show *XX TV*.

Just as I thought, their expressions became curious and expectant.

"Excuse me, but what year are you now?"

They looked at each other. The girl to the left opened her mouth. "We're seniors."

I'd guessed right. I smirked in my mind. "Do you have a little time right now? I'd like to ask you two something."

"Uh, what kind of thing?" It was, of course, the left one.

"There's a senior called Chiharu Katsuragi, isn't there? Are you aware that her older sister has gone missing?"

"Oh yeah, I know. Everyone at school is talking about it."

"I've heard that Miss Katsuragi is taking time off from school—is that true?"

The girl on the right side said something into the ear of the other girl. Their expressions were quite different from before. In other words, they became extremely cautious.

"We're in a different class, so…" the girl on the left said and returned my business card. "We were warned not to go babbling."

"Ah…then could you just tell me which senior class she was in?"

But waving their hands, they walked past me with quick steps.

After that, I used the same method to talk to three other girls, but the results were similar. I found out that Chiharu Katsuragi was in Class 2, but they ran away before I could ask anything else. It seemed the school had anticipated press initiatives and issued strict warnings to the student body.

I could get into trouble if the school found out that I was acting suspiciously in its vicinity. But there was something I just needed to know for certain.

I decided to move to Meguro station. It was a private school, so most of the students probably had to commute by train. I could see at a glance which school they came from by their uniform.

At a convenience store, I quickly spotted a girl. She was tall with long hair and was reading a magazine. I approached her from the side and said, *Excuse me.*

The girl furrowed her brow as she looked at me. She wasn't even trying to conceal her suspicion. *This one might be impossible*, I thought. I decided to drop my earlier tactic.

"I'm someone who's researching the disappearance of Nissei Automobile's executive vice president's daughter. Do you have time to talk?" I said in a low-key, professional tone.

I saw a change in the longhaired girl's face. She lowered her guard and even looked interested.

"What have you learned about it?" she asked me in turn.

"Well, not much... The police are being stingy."

"I see." The girl looked down at the floor.

"Umm, are you and Chiharu..."

"We're in the same class."

I nodded broadly. Luck was on my side. I'd somehow manage to achieve my goal.

"Can we talk somewhere quiet? Even five or ten minutes is enough. Oh, this is me." I showed the same business card as before.

"You're from a TV station? I don't think I can tell you anything special, though."

"That's okay. You can just tell me about Chiharu."

She glanced at her cellphone. It seemed she was checking the time. She closed the flip phone with a snap and nodded. "I have half an hour."

I thanked her.

There was a fast food place next to the convenience store, so we went in there. We sat near a window on the second floor. The girl with long hair had a frozen yogurt. Coffee again for me.

According to her, it seemed Chiharu did start taking time off from school around when Juri had run away from home. The school only said she was sick and didn't give details about her condition.

"Our homeroom teacher told us she wasn't feeling well and would be taking time off for a while. I don't think he knows what kind of illness it is either. Even when I went to ask him later in the staff room, he shook his head saying he didn't know. I don't think it was an act."

"Has your teacher tried contacting Miss Katsuragi's home?"

"He might have, but they must not have told him. Because the truth is that she's bedridden from the shock of her sister going missing, right? It would have been hard for her parents to say that. It seems like at that point they were hiding that her sister was gone," the girl said, scraping at the frozen yogurt with her spoon and eating some. Her pink tongue peeked out of her lips now and then.

"Are you close to Chiharu?"

"I think we're pretty close. I've gone to her house to hang out a few times."

"Then, have you met Juri before?"

"I haven't. Actually, this is just the first time I've heard of Chiharu having an older sister. She hadn't said a word about it before. Even when I asked her other friends, they said the same thing. Don't you think it's weird? So when I heard her sister was missing, I didn't know what to make of it. But Chiharu had such a shock from it that she's bedridden. She must love her big sis."

I didn't comment on that. I had my own interpretation, but I didn't think this girl needed to hear it. "Have you seen Chiharu since she started taking time off?"

"I haven't. I called wanting to go visit her, but her mom turned me away."

"Turned you away? What did she say?"

"Chiharu wasn't home and was recuperating at some facility far away. Even if I went to her house, I wouldn't be able to see her."

"Facility... Did you ask where it was?"

With her spoon still in her mouth, the girl shook her head. "I didn't. It seemed like she didn't want anyone visiting her, so I lost interest, too."

I nodded. I could understand the longhaired girl's reaction.

"Hey, would you have a photo of Chiharu?"

"Of Chiharu? I don't have one now, but I think I might at home."

"Where is your house? If I come with you, will you let me see them?"

The girl furrowed her brow again and cast me a suspicious look.

"I'm not sure I should be doing that without permission."

"Just looking at it is enough. I won't ask you to lend it to me, and I'll give it back to you on the spot."

"Then why do you want to see it? Chiharu doesn't have anything to do with her sister's disappearance."

She had a point. It wasn't like she trusted me. "I'm thinking of meeting with Chiharu. Before doing that, I should find out what she looks like. If I don't know her face, then I can't go looking for her."

I thought it wasn't a very persuasive answer, but it seemed the longhaired girl accepted it. After nodding, she asked me to wait for a bit, then took out her cellphone.

"What are you doing?"

"One sec."

She started composing a message. I drank the terrible coffee.

When she was done, she looked up and asked, "Is it true that Chiharu's sister got kidnapped?"

I almost choked. "Who's been saying that?"

"Everyone's secretly talking about it. That she's actually been kidnapped."

"I wonder where that rumor came from."

"I'm not sure. But somehow it's been spreading. Is it true?"

"The police haven't announced such a fact. They haven't told the press, to say the least."

"Isn't it that thing? A whatever agreement."

"Ah, an intermedia agreement? I don't think so, but the higher-ups might know something."

"But even if it were a kidnapping, if she hasn't come home in over ten days…" After saying that much, she cast down her eyes. "Forget it. I'm scared of saying something awful and having it come true."

I immediately understood what she was trying to say. It wasn't the kind of thing you wanted happening in real life.

Her cellphone went off.

"Ah, that was fast," the girl said.

"Huh?"

"Chiharu's pic. I just asked my friend to send it to me. That friend has a scanner or something, so she scanned a photo of Chiharu and sent it."

"I see…" Honestly, I was astonished. High school girls had a leg up on your usual businessman when it came to utilizing such tools.

"There you go." She turned her cellphone towards me. A girl smiled at me from a LCD display that was just a few inches large.

I had foreseen it, but the impact I felt still wasn't small. Somewhere inside of me, I wanted to disprove my own hypothesis. But what was on the screen made everything fact.

Displayed there was Juri's face. It was the girl who'd participated in a game with me until just days ago.

Even after I got back to the company, I couldn't concentrate on anything. I was in no shape to work, my hands full just organizing my disordered mind.

My theory had been right. The one who had appeared before me wasn't Juri Katsuragi, but her younger sister Chiharu. Chiharu had run away from home.

What I didn't understand was from there. Why had she said she was Juri? Was it simply on a whim? If so, why not tell the truth before embarking on a kidnapping game?

There were also too many things about the Katsuragis' reaction that were odd, starting with the father's. They must have known since receiving the first letter that the one who had been kidnapped was Chiharu and not Juri. Why hadn't they pointed out the mistake? Because the culprits mistaking the younger for the older sister didn't change the fact that their daughter had been kidnapped? Had they decided not to provoke the kidnappers needlessly?

There was just one thing that was clear. The fake Juri, in other words Chiharu Katsuragi, had returned home. She wasn't missing. The family was telling people that Chiharu was recuperating, so perhaps she was somewhere else, but she seemed to be under the Katsuragis' protection.

The one who was missing was the real Juri. And I hadn't ever met that Juri.

Where had Juri Katsuragi disappeared to?

The foreboding words the girl with long hair had uttered came back to me. I shook my head. Whatever might have happened, it wasn't my doing. The girl I'd dealt with was Chiharu.

Another ten days passed. I was still in turmoil. Neither the papers nor the nightly news reported any new developments regarding Juri Katsuragi. My honest wish was for things to stay that way. If I could have, I would have stormed into the Katsuragi residence and yelled at them to let me see Chiharu. I'd grab Katsutoshi Katsuragi by the collar and interrogate him about what on earth he was up to.

I wasn't getting much sleep. It was morning, but I writhed in my sheets. It was time to rise and shine, but my head felt incredibly heavy. I tried out excuses to take the day off.

But the phone ringing roused me even in that state. It rang without mercy, and I dragged myself out of bed to pick up the receiver.

"Yes, hello."

"Sakuma? It's me, Kozuka."

"Ah, did something happen?"

"Judging by how groggy you sound, I assume you haven't watched the morning news yet. Try tuning in. Once you get the situation, call me." With that, he hung up.

Scratching my head, I turned on the TV. A morning news program was playing. The male newscaster was saying something. *Juri*, I heard, and my eyes opened wide. I turned up the volume.

"This morning, in Yokosuka, the body of what is thought to be a young woman was found. From the fingerprints and other identifiers, it is believed that the woman is Juri Katsuragi, the elder daughter of Mr. Katsutoshi Katsuragi, the executive vice president of Nissei Automobile. She had gone missing about twenty days ago—"

20

Juri Katsuragi's overnight vigil was being held at a Buddhist temple about fifteen minutes by car from the Katsuragi residence. Many of us at Cyberplan were there to help and to offer incense, me among them. Naturally, Nissei Automobile employees handled greeting people, dealing with the VIPs, and all the other important stuff. We were just acting as guideposts on the streets.

Because it was the vigil of Nissei Automobile's EVP's daughter, the temple premises were overflowing with guests making condolence calls. Even though there were five lines for offering incense, people were crowding out into the street. Those of us who had come to help wondered in hushed tones what the next day's funeral would be like if the vigil was this way.

There was a break in the callers, so we decided to rest in a room in the back. There was sushi and beer, but it wasn't as though we could wolf down food there. Kozuka instructed us Cyberplanners to limit ourselves to one glass of beer each.

"Mr. Katsuragi looks down, as one might expect," Sugimoto whispered. "During the incense offering, I took a peek at him, but it's the first time I've seen him this down. He always seems filled with confidence with his head held high."

"No wonder. His daughter died," responded another coworker. "And it's not a normal way to die either."

"I think he must have been prepared for it, but of course it must be a shock to hear it for real."

"Of course. Honestly, I thought maybe she'd already been killed, but when I actually saw the news, I was shocked, too."

"I wonder what kind of person the culprit is."

"Same here. Did he kill her knowing she was the daughter of Nissei's EVP?"

"Who knows? They aren't sharing any details with us," Sugimoto said. He glanced around and covered his mouth with his hand. "Apparently, this girl Juri who got killed wasn't the child of his current wife."

"Oh, that, I heard that too."

"Plus, she wasn't by his first wife."

"Huh, then whose child was she?"

"His mistress. He took her in and raised her."

"Wow, Mr. Katsuragi, of all people."

"It might be because I know that, but his wife doesn't seem half as crushed as Mr. Katsuragi. The troublesome child from his old flame died, so maybe she's sighing with relief."

At his words, my colleagues who'd been listening to Sugimoto let a chuckle slip. Kozuka didn't miss that.

"No unnecessary chatter. We're not the only people here."

Scolded, Sugimoto and the others ducked their heads.

I was a little surprised that they knew a little about the secret of Juri's birth. I'd assumed it was the Katsuragi family's biggest secret. Even the daytime shows were glossing over that part. The dynamic—fearing the wrath of a leading sponsor—was at work for the time being. But if Sugimoto and the others had heard about it, that meant the information had leaked from somewhere. Even Katsutoshi Katsuragi couldn't pull over the iron curtain once we were dealing with a dead body.

At any rate, I was stuck on Sugimoto's last line. Indeed, Juri's death must have streamlined the Katsuragis' complicated situation.

Of course, how the Katsuragis themselves saw it was a mystery.

Chiharu Katsuragi, the fake Juri, hadn't made an appearance at the vigil. No explanation was given for this, but they must have told relatives and close friends that she wasn't handling the shock well. She was even skipping school, so it wasn't as though that explanation wasn't persuasive.

However, I suspected there was a different reason Chiharu hadn't shown herself. In short, she didn't want to see me. What I might say to her scared her.

Katsutoshi Katsuragi, or rather, the Katsuragi family was hiding something. And they were plotting. That was something I didn't doubt.

Juri Katsuragi's remains had been on a hill on the Miura Peninsula. A local resident had found her buried in the ground. Despite the advanced state of decay, from a partial fingerprint, her dental impression, and so on, it became clear that she was the missing Juri.

It was judged to be a murder based on the traces of a sharp object piercing her heart and causing massive blood loss. Some of her clothes had been removed and they couldn't find her personal belongings.

The place where her remains had been unearthed was something I couldn't help thinking about. Wasn't it that spot? I'd been invited by Juri, no, Chiharu to that hill where you could see the stars so well. The news didn't give the precise location, but I felt it couldn't be anywhere but there.

If that was the case, then why had Juri's remains been there? Why had Chiharu wanted to go to that place with me?

It was right when I was finishing my beer. I felt someone's presence and looked to the side. Katsutoshi Katsuragi was standing at the entrance. He was staring.

When I turned to look at him, he averted his gaze. Then he came inside. Everyone in the room had noticed by then and was beginning to sit up straight.

"Ah, as you were. Please make yourselves comfortable. Please." With a restraining gesture, Katsutoshi Katsuragi looked around the room. Then he bowed. "Thank you for everything regarding my daughter. I truly am sorry for causing you trouble at such a busy time for your work. The police have promised to do whatever they can to apprehend the culprit. That day isn't far away, I trust. However, what has to do with my daughter has to do with my daughter and is a private matter of the Katsuragi household when all is said and done. The daily work of Nissei Automobile and its business partners absolutely cannot be obstructed by what has happened. Please, everyone continue with your various plans, without undue concern. I intend to resume work as quickly as possible as well. Thank you very much for today."

Katsutoshi Katsuragi bowed his head deeply once again.

Returning a bow like everyone else, I thought about Katsuragi's earlier gaze. He had been looking in my direction. No, without a doubt, he had been looking at me.

That night, accessing the internet and reading a flash news headline, I couldn't but gasp.

"Juri Katsuragi Actually Kidnapped," it said. I double-clicked with my trembling fingers.

According to a police spokesman, the disappearance of Nissei Automobile EVP Katsutoshi Katsuragi's first-born daughter, Juri, who was recently found dead, was in fact a kidnapping. The culprit had contacted the family shortly after her disappearance, but Mr. Katsuragi had refrained from notifying the police to avoid endangering his daughter. The ransom was paid, and a police investigation was launched, but the facts were withheld from the public for the sake of Juri's wellbeing—

I was dumbfounded in front of the computer screen for some time. Katsutoshi Katsuragi really hadn't notified the police. That meant those feints meant for our opponents, the police, during that elaborate ransom exchange were all for nothing.

Why had Katsuragi not told the police? The talk of keeping his daughter safe just wasn't credible. Juri and Chiharu changing places, Juri getting murdered—all of it had to be connected.

Katsuragi's gaze from the vigil was burned into my eyelids and wasn't going away.

That man knew that I was the kidnapper. Of course he did, having heard everything from Chiharu, no doubt. What was his aim?

When the next day came, reports with even more details flooded in. Communicating via the CPT Owners Club bulletin board, the ransom exchange on the Metropolitan Expressway, and almost everything else I had done started going public. The Nissei Mukojima branch manager, in particular, was all over TV getting interviewed. The Juri Katsuragi kidnapping and murder was the hottest topic around.

"What a guy." A coworker rapped his knuckles against the sports daily he was reading. "Three hundred million yen, they're saying. Even in this age, three hundred million is a lot of money. Just by making a few calls on a cellphone, he got his hands on that marvelously. This culprit has got a good head."

"Nah, he was just lucky," the guy who sat next to me said. "If the police had actually been on the case, it might not have gone so well. They're saying if they'd been notified earlier, things would have played out differently."

"Well, of course they'd say so. They're not going to say, 'With this method, the money would've been theirs, even if we were on scene.' I bet they're kind of glad they weren't notified in advance.

Imagine if they'd been notified and were totally staking places out and the ransom had been taken from under their noses. How'd they look? On that point, thanks to finding out only after it was over, no matter what clever methods the culprit used, the police aren't embarrassed or anything. Besides, the hostage is dead, so they can investigate without worrying about that."

"Hey, hey, you're being too loud."

The two were facing each other with grins.

I picked up the receiver. Looking at a number recorded on my cellphone, I placed a call. It connected to a direct work extension. "This is the local news section," a familiar voice said.

"Hello, this is Sakuma."

"Ah, Mr. Sakuma. It's me, Yuguchi. Thank you for taking the bill the other day."

"About that case—have you found out anything since then?"

"You mean about Juri Katsuragi." Yuguchi's tone grew less jovial. "It's gotten intense, hasn't it? I think those remains were found not long after we saw each other. Well, I kind of expected that she was dead. Our people on the case have been staying up working all night lately."

"Any results?"

"Dunno. The Katsuragis' guard is super-tight, so we probably haven't learned anything beyond what's being reported. I'll try asking later."

"I'm counting on you. And, sorry for this all of a sudden, but can you see me tonight?"

"Uh, that *is* very sudden."

"I'm supposed to see Mr. Katsuragi soon. I want to have as much info as possible."

"I understand. I'll work things out. Is the same place as last time good? I think I can hop over at around seven."

"Got it. Seven."

After putting down the receiver, I went over the call I had just made. Would it be my downfall? Had I said too much? Had he found it unnatural?

But I quietly shook my head. There was no point in worrying about it now.

I thought about how I would use my time until seven. There was no way I'd be getting any work done.

When I went to the café, Yuguchi was already waiting at a table by the window. He found me and raised his hand.

"Sorry for doing this when you're busy."

"No, it must be worse for you, Mr. Sakuma."

I ordered an iced coffee and leaned forward. "Well, about that thing."

"Yes. I asked around as much as I could about what we know. But please keep everything I say from now off the record. We don't want to be on Nissei Auto or the police's shit list."

"I understand. Do you think I'd do anything to compromise you, Yuguchi?"

"Well, of course I trust you, Mr. Sakuma..." Yuguchi pulled out a pocket notebook. "To cut to the chase, the police still haven't found a solid suspect. Their angle of attack is Juri's relationships, but no one who fits the description has surfaced."

"Do the police think it was someone she knew?"

"Well, the victim was an adult and not a kid. Their take must be that she wouldn't have followed someone she didn't know. There's the possibility she was abducted by force, but the culprit had decided on her as a target beforehand, so the police must view this anyhow as the doing of someone with some connection to Juri or the Katsuragis."

"But we're talking about the Katsuragis. Couldn't people looking to get the ransom have done it thinking any rich girl would work?"

"Of course there's that take, but they seem to believe the possibility is low."

"I wonder why."

"That's because"—Yuguchi looked around and lowered his voice a notch—"the hostage was murdered. Someone with no connection to the Katsuragis could have returned her after taking the money, provided that he hadn't shown his face to Juri. But that isn't what happened. The culprit had no intention of safely returning Juri from the start."

I got what he was saying. Supposedly, her remains were at least two weeks old. In other words, she had to have died just a few days after she'd gone missing.

"The method was coldblooded, so the investigators seem to think that it wasn't simply for the money but based on some kind of grudge."

"A grudge…"

I didn't know what to think about that. I certainly wanted to get back at Katsutoshi Katsuragi. Indeed, I'd come up with the game for that very reason. But that was only because a card called Chiharu had fallen into my hands. In the first place, I hadn't killed Juri Katsuragi. In fact, I'd never met her.

"Have the police gotten ahold of any clues?"

"It seems they have a few. For the ransom exchange, Mr. Katsuragi had spoken with the culprit several times over the phone, and they have a tape recording of that."

"A tape? He recorded it?"

"It seems so. He hadn't notified the police at that time, but he planned on contacting them as soon as Juri returned safely. He did his best to collect evidence on his own in order to aid the investigation."

That man would certainly try. Not having notified the police in the first place was the bigger surprise.

"What other evidence do they have?"

"When it comes to that, the police don't tell us everything, you see... Oh, right, right." Yuguchi looked at his notebook and covered his mouth with one hand. "It seems that Juri wasn't spared in the other way either."

"The other way?"

"She's dead, so maybe we shouldn't really care, but I mean her chastity."

"Ah..." I was too stunned to speak.

"They actually *are* keeping that out of the news. But it left behind significant evidence for the police. A man's pubic hair," Yuguchi said, lowering his voice further, "and his bodily fluids—apparently it was left behind. Well, of course, it must have been dry when they found it."

I felt my pulse quickening. It took all I had to keep my dismay from showing on my face.

"Was there other evidence?" My voice was too high.

"There seems to be, but it hasn't been made public. If I find out, I'll contact you."

"Thanks, please do." I gulped my iced coffee and steadied my breathing. "Why Yokosuka?"

"Huh?"

"Why was she found in Yokosuka? Why did the culprit bury her where he did? Have the police been saying anything about that? For instance, maybe they think that's where the hideout was?"

"I haven't heard anything about hideouts, but there's a rumor that the police have been canvassing for witnesses there."

"Canvassing?"

"It's simple. Basically, with a photo of Juri Katsuragi in hand, they're asking if people ran across her. The police aren't seeing Yokosuka as a place where the culprit went to bury the body but as the scene of the murder itself. So they're guessing that there's someone somewhere who witnessed Juri while she was alive."

"Why do they think so?"

"Well, I don't know." Yuguchi spread both his hands and shook his head.

After we said bye, I went straight to my condo and, after eating a simple meal, sat down at the computer. But even after it finished booting, I didn't budge for a while.

The jigsaw puzzle pieces that had been scattered around in my head until now were slowly starting to come together. There were many incomplete parts, but I could see the overall outline.

Sweat flowed from my temples. It was what you'd call a cold sweat. It was pretty hot and muggy, but there were goose bumps all over my body.

Imagining the shape of the completed puzzle, I was panicking. Believing it was impossible, I broke up the puzzle, trying to somehow put the pieces together into a different picture, but no matter how many times I tried, it ended up the same. *If* there wasn't a mistake in my reasoning.

I took a deep breath and slowly started typing. I prayed from the bottom of my heart that there was a mistake in my reasoning. But praying would get me nowhere. I had to do what I could.

Suddenly remembering something, I stood up. I went to my bedroom and approached the coat that I had left on the hanger. I stuck my hand into its inner pocket and took out what was inside. It was the thing that might become my lifeline.

I returned to my computer and got back to work.

The final task was to write an email. I thought about it for some time and started typing as follows:

Mr. Katsutoshi Katsuragi,

This is a grave matter. I request your urgent contact. You should be aware of the subject matter. Any method of contact is acceptable. You should know my identity, so I venture there is no need to give you my name. I have no objections to you calling me on the phone, either. But make sure the investigative authorities do not notice. You must understand that such attention would hurt us both.

I wish to fully resolve the current complex situation with a deal. If I am not contacted within the next two days, I will have to come to you.

From,

The person who had Chiharu Katsuragi

It was hardly good writing, but I was in no shape to worry over word choices or phrasings. After reading it over several times, I sent it to the address I had emailed several times. My heart was still beating fast.

I hadn't calmed down the next morning. I didn't know when he would call me, so even when I went to the bathroom, I couldn't let go of the cordless phone's handset. After I went to work, I kept my cellphone close to me, and since he might call my work phone, I tried not to leave my seat. I also incessantly checked my email. I checked the CPT Owners Club website, too.

But there was no communication from Katsutoshi Katsuragi. I even wondered if my identity escaped him, but that simply wasn't possible.

Still burdened with uncertainty, I went back to my condo. I was starting to regret sending the email.

I unlocked the door and entered my home. I felt like throwing myself on the sofa, but before that, I checked my answering machine. There was no message.

I sighed heavily and sat on the sofa. It was when I was about to turn on the TV.

The bedroom door opened, and Juri came in.

21

Juri, I muttered, then shook my head.

"Chiharu, I should say? I'm glad to see you, it's been a while."

"Turn off the TV." She sat down in the armchair.

I took the remote, turned off the TV. In the quiet room, silence reigned for some time. It became oppressive. Juri's, no, Chiharu's face was also stiff. She was trying not to look at me straight.

"You emailed Papa, didn't you?"

"I've been waiting for his answer. But I never thought you'd come," I said, then addressed a glaring issue. "How did you get in here?"

She brought out a key from her small bag. It looked like mine.

"The pitch was that it can't be duplicated," I noted.

"It's not a duplicate. It's the spare key you lent me."

I stretched my arm and opened my desk's drawer. I looked into the corner where I kept the spare key. "But it's here."

Chiharu grinned. "That's a fake."

"A fake?"

I took the key in the drawer and compared it to mine. The maker and the shape were the same, but when I looked closely, there were subtle differences in the pattern of the cuts.

"So you switched it out."

"You can get keys from the same maker anywhere."

"When did you obtain one?"

"All I did was receive it. Papa brought it close by."

"Your papa, huh?" I sighed. My whole body was going limp. "So every bit of it was your side's doing."

"Not every bit. Didn't you come up with the kidnapping game?"

"And it served you well."

"We seized our precious opportunity. My last chance to escape dire straits."

"Dire straits." I forced a smile. I wasn't actually so calm. "May I take a guess?"

She glared. With the same eyes as when she'd done it, I imagined.

Staring back into them, I said, "You killed Juri, didn't you?"

Chiharu didn't fret. She must have seen my answer coming. After the email I'd sent to Katsutoshi Katsuragi, father and daughter alike would have accepted that I grasped most of the truth.

"It wasn't deliberate," she said, terribly casually, like when you've caused a minor hassle for someone.

"I already get that. It wasn't premeditated. You either killed her impulsively or didn't mean to kill her, but she ended up dying. Otherwise..." I licked my lips. "You wouldn't have run away from home that night."

"Right." Chiharu raised both her arms and stretched. "Ah, this does me good. I wanted to hurry up and tell you. Even the whole time I was here pretending to be Juri, I was just itching to talk. I wanted to see the surprise on your face."

"That bit was true, then."

"Which bit?"

"You said you ran away because you had an argument with Chiharu about some cosmetic cream. You probably did get into a fight. What was different was how it played out. Chiharu, who always hated Juri, stabbed her—isn't that right?"

With a sulky look, Chiharu turned her face away. I noticed how similar the shape of her nose looked to Katsutoshi Katsuragi's. Juri's nose in the photo was less flat and better shaped.

"What did you stab her with?"

"Scissors."

"Scissors?"

She swept up her hair. "I'm good at doing haircuts. Occasionally I even cut my friends' hair. So I had a beautician I know give me a pair."

"I see, and those scissors were in the washroom. When she used your cosmetic cream without asking, you had an argument, and you ended up stabbing and killing her with them."

"That cream," Chiharu said with a distant look, "is something I bought when I went to France with Mama. You can't buy it in Japan, and I was so careful in using it. But without even asking me, that bitch—" She looked straight at me. "She was the one who got physical first, though. She slapped my cheek."

"But it was certainly excessive self-defense. So, you stabbed and killed her, and scared, you ran."

Chiharu shot a glare at me then stood up. "I'm thirsty. Can I have something?"

Before I could reply, *Go ahead*, she had gone into the kitchen. When she came out, she was holding a bottle of white wine. Muscadet Sur Lie. It went well with light hors d'oeuvres.

"Can I drink it?"

"As you like."

"You'll have some, too, won't you?"

Before I could respond, she placed two wine glasses on the center table. She held out the corkscrew and the bottle to me.

"What were you going to do, running away? At that point, you were looking for a hotel room. After staying a night, what were you going to do?"

"Stop jabbering and focus on opening the wine, please."

I pulled the cork and poured wine into the two glasses. With only a gestured toast, we held the Muscadet in our mouths. It had a pleasant acidity and the signature *sur lie* fragrance of young grapes.

"I hadn't decided," she said.

"Huh?"

"I said I hadn't decided what to do. But I didn't want to be in that house. It was going to get crazy for sure, and they'd find out soon enough that I'd done it, and getting asked all sorts of questions by all sorts of people would be so annoying. And I hoped Papa or Mama would do something once they realized the culprit was me. I thought I'd go home after they'd cleaned up the mess."

"So you thought they'd secretly dispose of the body and see to it that you weren't arrested for murder." I drained the remaining wine in my glass and poured out more. "How selfish."

"I knew it was selfish. Even Papa wouldn't be able to squash a murder—I thought that, too. Didn't I just tell you that I was in dire straits?"

"And that's when I showed up."

"It's not like I asked you to. You're the one who approached me."

I had no reply to that. I had accosted her, indeed, hoping to get the dirt on Katsutoshi Katsuragi. "Why did you choose to follow me, though? *I can use this guy*—is that what you thought?"

Wine glass in hand, she shook her head. "Honestly, at that point, I didn't give a damn about anything. Including you. My head was filled with what I'd done, and I needed somewhere to stay for the time being, but I didn't want to go home. In other words, I didn't have any options then."

"Fine, you've convinced me." I drank my wine again. "Why did you pretend to be Juri?"

"The reason was simple. I didn't want to offer up my name. I didn't want a stranger knowing that Chiharu Katsuragi was wandering around being weird. It was just a lie I came up with on the spot."

I swayed my head from side to side. "It may have been a quick lie, but from then on, whenever you talked about yourself, you did so flawlessly as Juri. You know, you're quite an actress."

"It's probably sarcasm, but thanks."

"So then." I put my glass on the table. "When did you plan all this? Naturally, it must have been after I proposed the game, but it couldn't have been right then."

"It wasn't spontaneous or anything." She took the wine bottle in hand and tried to fill my glass.

"Hey, pouring wine is the man's job." I took it over and did it myself.

"Your game was a hint. 'He thinks I'm Juri. He wants to act like he kidnapped her.' I wondered if I could use that somehow. I believed I could. So for the time being I went along with it."

"And as you heard my plan, that conviction deepened?"

"I was convinced," Chiharu replied with a grin, "when Papa praised me."

"Praised you?"

"Right after hearing about the game from you, I decided to go ahead and call Papa. Also, Juri was on my mind."

"So you were in touch with him from when the game started. Well, why wouldn't you be. Mr. Katsuragi must have been rattled. I mean, his daughter had been murdered, and the killer was his daughter. He couldn't go to the police."

"For his part, Papa was trying to figure out if there was a way to cover it up. That's when I called. He seems to have been worried that I'd committed suicide. He sounded relieved to hear my voice. He didn't scold me about killing Juri. He told me to count on him to do something about it and to hurry up and come home. So I told him about you and your game."

"And he praised you."

"About intuiting that I could use your plan. According to Papa, it's having the intuition and decisiveness at clutch moments that divides the winners from the losers."

Thinking it was something Katsutoshi Katsuragi would say, I nodded. "And what instructions did Mr. Katsuragi give you?"

"First he told me to do as you say. Then he told me to report what that was in detail to him. Once the course of action was decided, he'd contact me."

"Contact you? How?"

"He'd call me on my cellphone," she said as though it were nothing.

"Cellphone? But didn't you not have one?"

"I did. You think I'd ever forget something so important?" Chiharu laughed heartily, mockingly at me. "But I kept it turned off while I was with you."

"I got played." I shook my head. "He gave you a whole bunch of instructions through that cellphone then. Going to Yokosuka, too? You don't have a friend called Yuki. Am I right?"

"I did. We were friends in middle school. Haven't seen her at all lately."

"You wanted me to go to Yokosuka because you planned on burying Juri's remains on a hill there. But making me go wasn't enough. Thinking ahead, you used all kinds of tricks to make sure I'd leave traces in Yokosuka."

"Yes. All kinds." Chiharu crossed her legs and looked at me with upturned eyes. "Can you guess?"

"While I was waiting for you, I was at the restaurant. Someone played a prank on my car while it was in the parking lot. The staff might remember my face. That it was an unusual car like the MR-S probably also left an impression. If the police went asking around with my photo, the staff would provide testimony. Was that prank the work of Mr. Katsuragi?"

"The one who did that was Mama."

"Your mama? I see, so you had one more accomplice."

"There are other traces of you, too."

"I know. But I don't get it." I looked her in the eye and proceeded to gaze at her crossed legs. "To obtain traces of me, you slept with me? Because you wanted my semen and pubic hair... I can't imagine that your parents pushed you to go that far."

"What Papa told me was to get my hands on your body hair. Do you remember there was a small statue on that hill? He told me to hide it there. But I thought it wouldn't be enough. Papa must have thought it'd be better with your semen. He couldn't ask me to do that, so he said your hair. I saw that, so I exercised my own judgment to obtain the absolute physical evidence we needed."

"Even though it meant having sex with a man you didn't care for."

"Are you sulking?"

"Not really."

"I did care for you. You're gutsy, and you've got brains. I didn't mind sleeping with you. If you'd been dumber and a lame bastard, I don't think I'd have been able to go that far."

"Is that supposed to be a compliment?"

"Papa also has a high opinion of you. It was crucial for our plan that you weren't stupid. If you were the type to come up with a sloppy kidnapping game, that would spoil everything. Papa suddenly went to your company, right?"

"Now that you mention it..." He had come asking to see games birthed by Cyberplan.

"His aim was to see a game you'd produced. *The Mask of Youth*, right? It seems after seeing it, Papa felt that you could be trusted."

I sighed and shook my head. I couldn't but let out a weak laugh. "So that's when he buys me?"

"When you had me call from the love hotel, you beautifully

worked in the sound of the whistle, remember? He said that was astute, too."

"And it was another trace." I had happily run along the rails that Katsutoshi Katsuragi had set for me.

"But the real match was from there. Papa really wanted to know how you were going to get your hands on the ransom. But you wouldn't even tell me. I almost couldn't resist telling you that no one had gone to the police."

"Mr. Katsuragi must have been so irritated by my Hakozaki feint."

"He was hoping you'd just take the money. But in the end he was impressed. He admitted that checking if there was a police tail was necessary."

"Did he say anything about the real ransom exchange?"

"Of course he said it was splendid. That way, there'd be almost no evidence to specify the culprit, and he thinks it would've gone well even if there had been a police tail or stakeout."

I nodded. I could hardly be pleased about it now, but at least it hadn't been a plan that earned Katsutoshi Katsuragi's derision. "We went to Yokosuka again with your two hundred seventy million yen. To hide the money in Yuki's room, which doesn't exist. What did you really do with the money?"

"I hid it in what looked like a storage room in that building. Then, I called Papa asap. After we left, he recovered it right away."

"I see. With that, Juri Katsuragi had been safely kidnapped and the ransom was paid. But there's one big problem. Well, I have a guess about the answer, though."

"What is it?"

"What were you planning on doing with me?"

Chiharu shrugged her shoulders. "That's a hard question for me to answer."

"It would be."

"You said you can guess? Well, let me hear it."

"You won't just tell me, even at this late date? Fine, fine. So, you've safely concealed Juri's murder, the staged kidnapping's been successful. But you have a small problem. Or should I call it a point of concern. It's that you probably can't keep me deceived. As the case gets reported, I sense the truth of the matter. In the worst case, I rush to the police, but you probably don't need to worry about that. As the principle offender in the staged kidnapping, I don't dare to. Yet you doubt that I'll keep mum. Moreover, if I come to the police's attention by some chance, I might confess. They might not believe me at first, but they'll investigate to see if there's any substance to it. The press will get in on the action. Nothing about that situation is welcome to the Katsuragis. There's pretty much only one way to solve it."

An alarm went off inside of me when I got that far.

Because there indeed was a stabbing pain in my head all of a sudden. It was spreading to my whole cranium. The pain actually began to subside, but I realized my senses were dulling at the same time. My consciousness was getting sucked into something.

I glared at Chiharu. Then I looked at the wine bottle.

"Thanks for that."

"Is it working?" She peered into my face.

"What did you put in the wine?"

"I don't know. Some drug that Papa gave me. I injected it into the bottle with a syringe beforehand."

Some kind of anesthetic, I thought with my groggy head.

"Did you mean to kill me from the start?"

"I don't know. I just do what Papa tells me to do."

"He's been meaning to kill me. Otherwise, this plan falls apart. That man wouldn't devise an incomplete plan."

I tried standing up, but my body wouldn't obey me. I stumbled and slid off the sofa. The table corner struck my side, but it didn't hurt.

"I just did as I was told. I don't know what happens afterwards. Because Papa will take care of everything."

Chiharu stood up. It seemed she'd just been pretending to drink the wine.

I was starting to lose consciousness. Everything before me was growing hazy.

I couldn't blank out. If I did, they'd continue with their plan. In other words, they'd kill me and make it look like a suicide. Would the motive be that I couldn't endure the weight of my crime? Or maybe I'd seen the writing on the wall and thought that my arrest was a matter of time.

"...Wait," I squeezed out. "Listen to me. It's best...if you listen."

I couldn't tell where Chiharu was. I wasn't even sure if she'd heard me. Even so, I focused all my nerves into my throat.

"The computer. My automobile park...file..."

I tried moving my mouth, but the commands from my brain didn't reach it. I realized that my voice was failing me. Perhaps it was my sense of hearing. But really, it made no difference. It was as though darkness were enfolding my brain. I tasted what it was like to hurtle down an incredibly deep hole. *This might be my last sensation ever*, I thought.

I felt suffocated as though something were sitting on my chest. I wondered if I'd had a terrible nightmare. My face was hot. Yet I felt chilly below my neck. No, "cold" was more like it. I realized I'd broken out into an intense cold sweat.

I had my eyes closed. I was relieved that I could still sense that. I'd somehow not been killed yet. I opened my eyes. It was blurry, but I could see something. It was extremely dim.

Slowly, my vision came back. It was my room as I remembered it. It seemed I was lying on the sofa. I tried moving my body and winced. A terrible urge to vomit and a headache descended upon me. It had such an impact that I nearly passed out again.

But after exhaling and inhaling repeatedly, the nausea and headache subsided a bit. I slowly raised myself halfway up. The vessels behind my ears were throbbing.

"It seems you're conscious," a voice came. A man's voice.

I tried looking around with just my eyes. I was feeling too sluggish even to move my neck.

Soon, the silhouette of a person appeared in the corner of my vision. The person sat down on a chair across from me. It was Katsutoshi Katsuragi.

I fixed myself into a sitting position on the sofa. My body was still unsteady. If he tried to attack me, I didn't think I could defend myself adequately. But Katsutoshi Katsuragi didn't seem to care as he leisurely crossed his legs and lit a cigarette.

He was wearing a double-breasted suit. That gave me more peace of mind. If he intended to kill me, he would have dressed down in order to keep a low profile.

"The main actor finally makes his appearance," I said, my own voice sounding muffled to me. "Or should I say the mastermind in the shadows."

"Thanks for looking after my daughter," Katsutoshi Katsuragi said. His tone was calm.

I looked around. "Did your dear girl go home?"

"I sent her on ahead so my better half wouldn't get worried."

"It seems your wife is also an accomplice."

Without responding to that, Katsutoshi Katsuragi stared at me. "I believe you've heard the gist of it from my daughter. I intended to explain it to you myself, but she said she had to see you one last time."

"I'm glad I got to see her, too. I don't know if it will be the last time, though."

"I should first thank you for your trouble. I'm not being sarcastic. I believe you've already heard it from my daughter, but you did extremely well. I could even say perfectly. Was that method for obtaining the ransom your original idea? Or did you borrow a page from some piece of detective fiction?"

"I thought of it."

"I see. It was impressive." He slowly breathed out cigarette smoke. He looked at me from behind the drifting screen. "However, it's not as though there aren't parts that I must find fault with. Partway through, you started instructing me in English, but a policeman or two might have been quite fluent in it. I can't give you a perfect score on that."

"I knew that you're also conversant in French, and I can speak a bit of it. But I decided against it because it would narrow down the criminal profile. In today's Japan, millions speak English, but not so for French. It was a conclusion I came to after weighing their respective risks."

"Ah, then let's agree to disagree." Katsutoshi Katsuragi didn't seem to my mind my objection.

"Your own plan was impressive, too. It relied on your daughter's star turn, but I admire how you buried and planted so many things in advance amidst all the constraints."

"Come on, it's nothing compared to operating a business. This time I just needed to fool you, but leading a company requires fooling countless people—employees, consumers," the executive vice president averred with a straight face. He took a drag from his cigarette. "By the way, it seems you asked my daughter a question."

"Yes, about what you plan to do with me."

Katsutoshi Katsuragi grinned and dropped his cigarette ash into the ashtray. He uncrossed his legs and nodded, pleased.

"Even if the whole plan went well, our family couldn't have peace of mind. Because there is one person who knows our whole secret. Shunsuke Sakuma—what to do about him. We could make it seem like he'd committed suicide and have the police believe that he'd kidnapped Juri Katsuragi. The final polish. You inferred that my blueprints involved your demise."

"Was I wrong?"

"I won't say you were. It would be a lie to say that I never considered it. But dear Sakuma. I'm not that simplistic. I'm a little miffed that you thought so. Not that I don't understand your point of view. Your perfect plan ends up being your trap; anybody would feel insecure. That's why you thought to arrange a means to protect yourself. Well, you really were the man I hoped you were." Katsutoshi Katsuragi cast his eyes behind me. My computer sat there. I could hear the fan, so it seemed to be on.

"Did you see the file?"

"I did, of course."

The words I'd spoken to Chiharu the moment before I lost consciousness hadn't been uttered in vain.

"When I heard from Chiharu that there was some kind of file, I made light of it, thinking it couldn't be anything serious. I assumed what would be in there was a text document describing the truth of the incident along with a warning that the data would make its way to the police in the event of your death."

"Wouldn't even that give you pause?"

"Why? All I'd need to do is deny it. If we intended to kill you, we wouldn't be hindered by such a trifle. I would simply assert that the kidnapper had made up a story before committing suicide. Whom do you think the police would believe?"

I didn't answer, to indicate that I had no desire to refute him. With a satisfied smile, Katsutoshi Katsuragi took his time putting out his cigarette in the ashtray.

"But you weren't that incompetent. There was a letter about the truth of the incident just as I had predicted, but also another file.

Even I was amazed by that. Or maybe I should say I was floored."

"To confess, it was a fluke," I came clear. "I didn't think at the time that it would serve such a purpose."

"Brilliant people are like that. Without even meaning to, they gather materials to reinforce their position. You can't teach that sensibility."

I flashed a wry smile. I hadn't foreseen being praised by this man in such a manner.

"I didn't intend to kill you," Katsutoshi Katsuragi said. "Because there is no need to kill you. You wouldn't tell anyone what really happened as long as the police don't catch you. And I have no worries about you getting caught. Because we'll cover for you. As the victims, we will be able to produce as much evidence as needed that you couldn't have been the culprit. Of course, that was contingent on having you complete the game perfectly. It goes without saying that you did."

"If there was no need to make it seem like I was the culprit, why did you need to make sure that I left traces in Yokosuka?"

"For one thing, I needed you to be vulnerable. Evidence that I could always use to finger you as the culprit would place you in such a predicament. But what I really needed were traces of *a* culprit. That the kidnapping had been staged absolutely must not come to light. To indicate that a culprit did exist for sure, I needed a real culprit acting."

"Then, why did you put me to sleep just now?"

Katsutoshi Katsuragi grinned. His expression said he'd been waiting for the question. "Did you think you'd be put to death if you fell asleep?"

"If I'm truthful."

"Right. So you marshaled the last ounce of your strength to pull out your trump card. What I wanted to see was exactly that. The last card you would flash."

I grunted. "You wanted me to show you my hand?"

"The game is over. But we didn't have a winner yet. I showed you my whole hand. What remained was what cards you had."

Katsutoshi Katsuragi glanced at the computer again. At his lead, I also turned around. I looked at the monitor.

It displayed a photo. It was clear to anyone that it was a photo of this room.

Chiharu from when she had been calling herself Juri was carrying a tray with a meal she had made for me.

ABOUT THE AUTHOR

Keigo Higashino was born in the lowest of lowly ghettos in Osaka, to poor parents, in a tiny house that in his words was "always one room short." He lived off hand-me-downs, and from girls at that. Always lonely, he took to reading massive amounts of fiction—anything he could get his hands on.

An engineer by training, he became a full-time writer when his *After School* won the Edogawa Rampo Prize in 1985. His stateside debut came when *Naoko* was translated and published by Vertical, Inc. in 2004. Mr. Higashino's fame in North America has only grown since. *The Secret*, the film adaptation of *Naoko*, was remade with David Duchovny, while *The Devotion of Suspect X* (from Minotaur Books) was nominated for the Mystery Writers of America's Edgar Award in 2012. *The Name of the Game Is a Kidnapping* also spawned a theatrical feature, *g@me*.